DEDICATION

For the rule breakers.

A.D. BRAZEAU

Murder in the Lightning Room

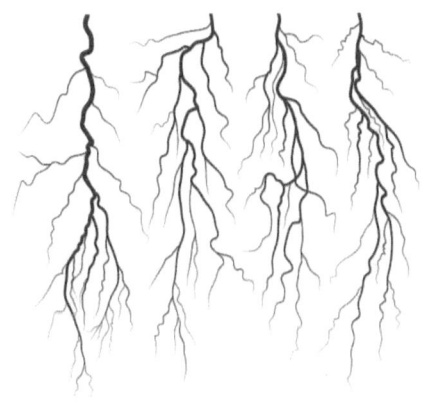

A.D. Brazeau

Murder in the Lightning Room
Copyright © 2022 A.D. Brazeau
All rights reserved.

ISBN: (ebook) 978-1-958136-01-0
(print) 978-1-958136-02-7

Inkspell Publishing
207 Moonglow Circle #101
Murrells Inlet, SC 29576

Edited By Yezanira Venecia
Cover art By Fantasia Frog Designs

CHAPTER ONE

Colorado Springs, 1899

The body on the flagstone lay at an odd angle. The man's left arm was unnaturally bent behind him, his back twisted. Other than my father, resting in quiet repose, I'd never seen a dead body outside a casket at a funeral. I stood frozen to my spot, staring at the crumpled figure.

There was glass on the walkway, blood pooling around the man's head. I'd never seen anything so grotesque.

What do I do?

A woman's scream, loud and piercing, snapped me back to reality. An older lady, tiny like a bird, ran down the front steps of the boarding house. She bent over the man on the ground.

"I'll get the police," I called out. I tried to turn but was tripped up by the hem of my dress. I took hold of my dress, and my swift feet carried me across the street. The county jail wasn't far. In a town where nothing ever happened, I should easily find some help.

My uneventful morning of house calls with the city's dowagers had turned dramatic in an instant. I wasn't quite ready to think on what I had seen, so I pushed the ugly vision from my mind, running down the side of the wet road.

A policeman stood outside the jail, milling about as he seemed to enjoy the shining sun on this cold morning. I was about to change his day for the worse. A few men in suits, no doubt from the bank, gawked as I raced by. Society girls were not often seen barreling toward officers of the law.

I stopped shy of ramming into the squat man. "Sir, please come with me. There's been a terrible accident." I gasped, the words rushing out in a tumble.

The officer, startled at first, recovered himself with aplomb. "Lead the way," he said, his breath moving the fine hairs of his long mustache.

If the two of us speeding back toward the boarding house appeared odd to the town's residents, I couldn't be bothered to notice. I ran ahead, holding up my long skirts until I stood on the very spot I had only moments before. A small crowd now gathered around the dead man and the bird-like woman who sat on her knees next to the corpse. The officer left me where I rested to take command of the situation.

I remained for a moment. I wanted to help, but what more could I do? I hadn't seen the man fall, and I hadn't heard anything, either. As I stood watching the officer direct people, some heathen honked the horn of his motor car, startling two horses pulling a buggy in front of him. As I seemed forgotten in the chaos, and with no other options, I went about my business. Staring was distasteful.

I shivered in the early morning air. Winter would come early this year. There was already a fine dusting of snow on Pikes Peak, visible in the distance behind the house where tragedy had occurred. The blue and white of the mountains drew my eye. The dead man would never look on it again. My chest tightened at the thought.

It was a view I, too, was in danger of losing. I would, if all went according to my plan, be leaving soon to further my education. Mother wanted me to attend Colorado College, mere blocks from home. I wasn't so sure I wanted to. I wished to travel, to see more of life than our small, comfortable world afforded.

But in that instance, part of me wanted nothing more than to go home and crawl back into bed; the incident with the dead man left a bad taste in my mouth. However, Mr. Hill wouldn't be happy if I were late to class, no matter the circumstance, so I hurried on, all the while thinking, *Who was the poor man? How could he have ended up as he did?* Whatever happened, I hoped he hadn't suffered.

Walters, our stableman, waited a block away with the buggy. As I rounded the corner, the scent of afternoon coffee wafting from the café, he caught me in his eye. There was disapproval written all over the lines of his forehead. He continued to watch me with a scowl until I stood in front of him.

Walters was a tall man, in no way bent from his many years of work in the carriage house. His back was as straight as any twenty-year-old's, and his hair, though white, was full and thick.

"Miss Cora," he began, "you're going to be late. We better get a move on."

He held out a steady arm as I climbed into the back of the transom. "I know, Walters. You'll never believe what happened. A man fell to his death from one of the boarding houses on Cascade. I had to run for help."

Walters stood with his hands on his hips, shaking his head. "That's a shame, Miss. Sorry you had to see it. Are you all right?"

I nodded, swallowing the knot I only then noticed forming in the back of my throat. It was a shocking sight to see. The woman's piercing screams along with the man's twisted and bloodied body would haunt my dreams. My mind wandered to the death of my father, of grasping his lifeless, cold hand; a hand that once was so warm and strong. Life was so quickly over and not always in the way we anticipated. Father hadn't expected for his heart to fail, and that man hadn't expected to slip from … well, from wherever he slipped from.

Walters alighted onto the driver's box and we were off. The cold air whipped around me as Walters and Lady, my favorite mare, made tracks to the school. We weren't far, but Mother hated when I walked in the mornings, as it was usually still dark when I left for school. Since I had visits to return today, I had started out a bit later.

I pressed myself into the back of the seat as far as I could, pulling the fur blanket over my shaking legs. The leaves, already falling, would be gone soon. The trees lining the streets, green and full in the summer, were days away from being stripped stark and bare for winter. I didn't mind the cold, but this weather made me feel bleak on the best of days. After witnessing such a scene on the street, this was *not* the best of days. Something felt off in this small city of ours.

CHAPTER TWO

Mr. Hill had lost his mind. "Tesla? *The* Tesla?" I stared at my teacher.

Has he gone mad?

The wooden chair I'd sat in for the last two hours was uncomfortable, but I had to finish our conversation.

"Yes, Cora. *The* Tesla." Mr. Hill paused, pursing his lips as if in thought. "Your studies here are coming to an end, and you said you wanted a challenge before college. There's no greater challenge I'm told than assisting Nikola Tesla in his lab." Mr. Hill chuckled, shaking his head at a joke only he understood.

The thought of working with and learning from a genius of Tesla's magnitude would be a dream come true. Tesla had been here since the beginning of the summer and probably wouldn't be here forever. His lab east of the city's center had drawn more than a few onlookers in its early days. The townspeople of Colorado Springs were enthralled by the famous man and his incredible work, as people were the world over.

Snow drifted past the windows. The flurries began about an hour ago. It was still light out, so I could see people outside, dressed against the weather, driving their buggies and riding their horses around the park, which stood like a little oasis in the center of town.

My brow creased. I pondered what Mr. Hill was saying. "Would he accept a female assistant?" I asked as I tucked stray tendrils of dark-brown hair behind my ear. There was a chill in the classroom. Desks were lined in long rows, chairs neatly pushed in. Chalk dust still hung in the air from the freshly wiped board and mingled with the scent of ink and paper. A great map of the world hung from the wall opposite the windows. I spent a lot of time gazing with dreamy eyes at the different countries and cities, wondering where I would travel first when my life began in earnest.

"Tesla seems to be unaware of things like gender. His only interest is his work. All you need to do is prove yourself capable, which I'm sure you will. He recently fired an assistant and needs a replacement as soon as possible. Think about what it is you wish to accomplish, Cora. Could this help you?" Mr. Hill extricated himself from the small half-desk, stretching his back as he did so.

He was looking stiffer, older, this year. His hair, which was dark when I first began at Colorado Springs High School, was now mostly white. His smooth skin still appeared youthful, though, and this made me smile. I knew he was likely exhausted from his day of teaching and would appreciate it if I went on home, so I stood, smoothing down the satin of my dark-blue day dress, gathering the rest of my things. "You know I wish to teach at a great college one day, sir. Even if this is a profession for men, it won't always be so. Tesla's name would help me open a few doors. The only thing I'm not sure of is the time commitment. Why don't you assist Mr. Tesla, Mr. Hill?"

My teacher smiled as he walked over to the brass coat rack. "Mrs. Hill thinks I'm away from home too much as it is. Besides, I can't stand for long hours anymore. Teaching is becoming a burden on my legs these days." He removed my knit scarf, passing it to me.

I took the scarf, wound it around my neck, and sighed.

"I'll think about it. I'm not sure I'd be any use to him. My interests are less in electrical engineering and more in biological sciences."

"Yes, I know. Still, it's a great opportunity, Cora. Think about it, but don't take too long. Another day or two and he'll be expecting his new assistant."

Mr. Hill held open my coat, and I turned around to slip in my arms. "One thing before you meet him, if you so decide. Tesla has a fair few eccentricities, not unusual for a man like him. Don't be alarmed. Take them in stride. He's intense but harmless."

I didn't find this comforting. In fact, this last bit of information set my mind even more resolutely against the idea. There were other ways to gain some experience before I began applying for colleges.

The frigid silk lining of my coat sent a shiver through my limbs. I knew the cold of the room was nothing compared to what I would feel when the icy wind hit my face outside. A little snow didn't scare me if it didn't get too deep. The fresh air would do me good, help me focus my thoughts, and when I arrived home, Willow would delight in a snowy romp.

"Thank you for taking the time to talk with me. I'll let you know what I decide."

Mr. Hill accompanied me to the outside. I tugged on my gray gloves as we walked.

"Cora, where is Mr. Walters with the buggy?" Mr. Hill looked up and down the street. The snow fell harder now, the giant snowflakes collecting on our shoulders and the tops of our hats. The feather in my silk bonnet would need replacing, that is if the hat was found to be salvageable.

"I told him not to come back for me. I wanted to walk home."

I had begged Walters not to come for me, but knowing he and Mother would both fret at the weather conditions, I wouldn't be surprised if I were to run into him along the way.

Mr. Hill's brow creased with worry as he now looked up into the sky.

"I'll be fine, sir. I love the snow, and the cold doesn't bother me." I pulled up the collar of my coat as far as I could. I realized I had made a mistake. The weather was worsening by the second, but I didn't want to give Mr. Hill too much time to worry over my predicament, so I began walking west toward home. "Goodnight, Mr. Hill. Stay warm." I laughed to relieve his anxiety and mine. Mr. Hill had only about one block to walk to his neat home on Boulder Avenue, whereas I had about two miles. I normally enjoyed the forty-minute walk when the weather was fine. This evening's stroll would prove more difficult.

I did enjoy the snow to a point, but I was a rational woman and knew I would be soaked through by the time I arrived home. As I walked parallel to the park, stubbornness took over. As long as I kept the flakes from slipping past the barrier of my scarf, freezing me like a block of ice from the inside out, I would be fine.

The sun began to descend. Within the hour, it would be falling away behind the snow-carved ridges of the Rocky Mountains. I would have liked to walk faster, but the sidewalks were wet and slick underneath my soles. My new boots were unlikely to survive the night. These were a gift from my mother, and their ruination would give her another reason to wish for a more socially glamourous daughter.

I fretted over my frigid predicament as I crossed Nevada Avenue and trudged toward Tejon Street. There was still quite a long way to go. I was certainly a fool to insist on walking. At the next corner, a buggy pulled up next to me, splashing me with slushy muck from the road.

"Yuck," I groaned.

"Cora, what on earth on you doing?" a familiar voice yelled down at me.

Snowflakes caked my lashes, making it difficult to see. I attempted to blink through the white fluff. Of all the people to come along at a moment like this, of course, it would be *him.*

Harrison Byrne was the most irritating boy in my year at school. Harrison moved to town less than twelve months ago and insisted on calling me Cora, rather than Miss Croft, as was polite. I frowned. "Walking, obviously, Mr. Byrne. If you don't mind, I've a long way to go and I'm already frozen to the bone."

I turned on my boot heel to leave. As I did so, my foot slid out from under me and I tumbled sharply onto the hard ground, hip first. A dull pain jammed its way into my back and down my leg. I moved to my other side in an attempt to rise when I felt strong hands take hold under my arms.

"Steady now. I bet that hurt." Harrison Byrne stood behind me, holding on to my arms, breathing down into my ear. I was sore but more annoyed with myself for falling in front of him. What frustrated me even more was that I needed and was accepting his help to stand. I squeezed my eyes shut, allowing Harrison to pull me up to my feet.

"I'm fine, thank you." I wanted to mention how I never would have fallen at all had he not distracted me, but I didn't quite have the energy. Instead, I massaged my hip.

"Good," Harrison breathed, again in my ear, sending a chill I didn't need down my spine. He continued to hold me by one arm around the waist. "Get in, I'll take you home."

Stubborn wasn't something I could afford to be in this situation. If I insisted on walking, I would never make it. Continuing to rub my hip, I sighed, stepping out of Harrison's protective grasp. "Yes, thank you. I'm sorry if I was rude before." I wasn't all that sorry, but I wanted more than anything to get in the buggy.

Harrison chuckled as he held out his hand for me to take. He helped me into the back of the open-air buggy. I would continue to get wet but would be home much quicker, so I wouldn't be such a fool as to complain. The well-used carriage belonged to Harrison, who drove people around after school for money. I didn't know much else about him, except that he lived with his family east of the center of town.

"Where am I taking you, Cora?" Harrison seated himself on the box and half-turned, one eyebrow raised, ginger locks sweeping his forehead. He had a look about him I wasn't sure I liked.

"I live on Wood Avenue, Mr. Byrne. Head north and I'll direct you as we go." A slow heat started to burn in my cheeks. I wanted nothing more than for Harrison to turn back around. This wasn't the first time he'd had this effect on me. More than once, I'd caught him staring at me when he should have been focused on Mr. Hill's lecture. Each time I had the same reaction.

After a moment too long, Harrison turned back to the large brown stallion, flicked his wrist, and clucked his tongue. As we drove, I observed him from behind. His pageboy hat wasn't doing much to keep the snow off his face and shoulders. His thick, knee-length canvas jacket seemed much more weather-resistant as the flakes of snow collected on the surface of the material without being absorbed.

"It was lucky for me you came along," I blurted out, upset with myself for not being able to sit in silence. I crammed a gloved hand into my mouth to stifle any further observations.

Harrison looked back. "It wasn't luck. I was on my way home and Mr. Hill flagged me down. Said you had some crazy notion of walking home in this mess."

I shifted in my seat. "Oh, I see. Well, I'm grateful to him and to you. I suppose I didn't think it was quite so bad."

We passed several businesses and homes lining the streets one after the next in almost perfect uniformity as we made our way out of the center of town. I looked up at the dull gray sky. The snow was picking up, along with the wind, coming down sideways in thick, cotton-like wisps. Pulling up my scarf around my ears, I settled further into the back of the seat. This was the most snow we'd had in a long while. The weather in Colorado was often unpredictable. My mother always said you could never get too comfortable, and just because the day began one way did not mean it would end the same.

I shook, the air against my wet skin like icy shrapnel to my senses.

"Almost there," Harrison called ahead.

I took a deep breath. I would soon be warm again. I peered around Harrison's body. Colorado College was a welcome sight. This meant we were close to home.

Harrison continued until we were finally trotting down Wood Avenue. The pleasant tree-lined street was quiet, smoke billowing from the chimney of every fine house we passed. The streets were double-wide so carriages could turn around.

"There it is!" I yelled, an octave too high. My voice cracked, betraying the excitement I felt to be at home. Composing myself, I continued. "The white house with the gray shutters."

Relief flooded my senses as the buggy came to a stop in front of my home. The imposing Queen Anne structure had been designed by my father, built for my mother as an anniversary gift. The steeply pitched roof was topped with an elaborately decorated gable on top of which had been erected a wrought-iron spire. As a child I always kept one eye on the thing, terrified the spire would break off and impale me. Conversely, the expansive wrap-around porch was lined with figure-eight-shaped posts I delighted in tracing with my hand while I raced around the perimeter, chased by my father as we played tag.

Without waiting for Harrison, I stepped out of the buggy, alighting onto the snow-covered cobblestone, my limbs shaking with cold. With trembling hands, I reached into my purse.

"No charge. The only payment I need is the knowledge I got you home safe."

Before I could respond, I heard the sharp voice of my mother behind me. "Cora Croft! Where on earth have you been in this blizzard? I'm sick with worry and was about to send Walters out to find you."

I turned to see Mother dressed for the evening meal in elegant black silk, rushing down the walk with nothing to cover her bare arms. My mother, Isabella, looked anything but sick. As usual, she glowed with life. Her wrinkleless skin was luminescent in the lamplight, every hair perfectly coiffed.

"I'm fine, Mother, coming in now." I swiveled around to say goodbye to Harrison as Mother moved alongside me and cut me off.

"Aren't you in Cora's class, young man?"

Harrison bowed slightly. "Yes, ma'am. Harrison Byrne." He touched his hat to take his leave. "Good evening, ma'am, Cora."

"Stop right there." My mother spoke in the parental tone of one who expects the complete attention of those around her. "You take that horse and buggy around to the carriage house. Walters will be there to help you. Then come inside to dry off and warm up."

Mother turned on her heel, taking my hand and dragging me along the snowy path. She wasn't going to take no for an answer, and Harrison wasn't giving one. As I was pulled along by my mother, I looked back to see Harrison maneuvering the buggy toward the back of the property. I wasn't sure how I felt about this. Surely it would be better if he made his way home.

The ground-floor windows of the house were ablaze with light, moisture gathering in beads on the thick panes. Mother led me inside as if I were a child, not releasing my hand until the imposing oak door was closed and we were standing in the hall. The air inside was so warm I wanted to cry.

A wagging tail, smiling mouth, and clear happy blue eyes greeted me as soon as I entered. "Hi there, baby," I said to my dog as she jumped at my legs. Willow, a black and white husky my father brought home as a puppy almost nine years ago from his travels in Russia, was my constant companion.

"Stand up straight, Cora. We need to get these things off you." Mother continued to treat me as a child. She unpinned my ruined hat and tossed it on the table as I wrestled off my wet gloves stuck to damp fingers.

"That was very irresponsible, Cora." She turned me toward her and began unbuttoning my sodden coat. "We'll be lucky if you don't come down with your death."

I gently pushed away my mother's hands. "I'll be fine, Mother. I shouldn't have sent Walters home, but I'll be okay. Promise."

Marsh, our ladies' maid, walked without producing a sound. She came up behind me, startling me out of my skin. "The dress will have to come off right here, Miss Croft. I cleaned the carpets upstairs this morning and won't have you trailing wet all over."

I groaned when I realized my quiet mother agreed with this pronouncement by her silence. Marsh laid an enormous cream-colored blanket on the carpet. Then the two women went to work getting me extricated from my dress. I looked around while they tugged and pulled, making sure there was no one else observing the scene.

When I stood in my petticoat, knickers, corset, and bustle, the air unpleasant on my bare arms, Marsh held up the blanket and enveloped me in its warm threads. I left the women to deal with my wet things and dashed up the stairs to my room, Willow at my heels. Warmth and solitude were all I craved.

Teeth still chattering, I crossed my deep, plush rug to fan open the blanket in front of the roaring fireplace. Willow made herself comfortable on the bed, curling up like a squirrel, her nose covered by her long, fluffy tail. The blast of heat was a balm to my frigid body. I stood there, blanket out like a cape, as long as I could.

"Dinner is about to be served, Miss Croft. Let's not keep cook or your mother waiting any longer than we need to."

I jumped again at the sound of Marsh behind me. Her

English accent was still strong after spending more than thirty years in America. I loved Marsh's voice as a child, begging her to read story after story, the cadence of her words lulling me always into a dreamlike state.

"Thank you for your help downstairs, Marsh. And …" I loved to tease Marsh. She would have everyone believe she possessed a heart of stone with her tough demeanor, but I knew she was tender under it all. "If I'm correct, I believe you were toasting this blanket in front of the fire for me."

Marsh harrumphed under her breath. "Figure you'd come in dripping wet," was all she said as she pulled a beaded crimson dress from the wardrobe.

I laughed as I crossed to Marsh and dropped a kiss on her cheek. "You know me so well." I raised my arms for her to drop the dress over the top of my body, my underpinnings quite dry.

As Marsh buttoned up the back, I leaned over for my silver-plated hairbrush, doing my best to smooth the stray, wet hairs back in place. I pinched my cheeks for color and was ready to join my mother in the dining room. My appearance in no way matched Isabella's, but it would have to do.

As I entered the darkly paneled room, the warmth from the fireplace enveloped me. It was fully dark outside now and the crystals from the chandelier sparkled with the light from the flames of a dozen candles. I moved toward my place next to Mother, who sat at the head of the table. The form of Harrison Byrne startled me. He sat opposite my chair, hands clasped in his lap.

I almost forgot him in all the chaos of the hallway. He rose as I sat, catching my eye. The familiar heat once again flamed in my cheeks. Once I was seated, Mother patted my hand. "Very good, dear. How do you feel?"

My mother insisted on coddling me, even though I was seventeen years old. I squirmed, trying not to sigh outwardly. "I'm fine, Mother."

She lifted the small crystal bell by her hand, ringing it

once to signal the family of two, along with their guest, was ready to eat. "Mr. Byrne was telling me about his day. How was yours, Cora? Did you stay after to talk with Mr. Hill again?"

"I did. He suggested I work at Nikola Tesla's lab as an assistant over the fall break," I said simply, bringing the crystal glass of red wine to my lips.

"What?" Mother's voice rang throughout the room. "Out of the question. I hope you told him no, Cora."

She was usually supportive of my endeavors, so this statement confused me. A slight reddish tint bloomed over her chest. I looked again, and the blush was gone. My tired eyes must have been playing tricks on me in the firelight. "I said I would think about it. Why would you not want me to? I could learn so much from him."

Mother sighed. She picked up the napkin already resting on her lap, fidgeting with it. I noticed her eyes slide toward Harrison then snap back to her lap. "Well," she began. "There's the shocking death of his most recent assistant. You may not have heard of it, as the poor man died this morning. The whole situation seems so strange."

My heart was in danger of stopping. The broken man I saw that morning was Tesla's assistant? The one he fired? I kept myself still, eyes trained on my plate. I played with the fringe of the lace tablecloth.

Mother continued, still fidgeting with her napkin. "Also, I've heard things about Mr. Tesla. He's an odd man, and I'm not sure it's a good idea for a young lady like yourself to work in such a close environment with him."

I met Harrison's gaze. The flickering light from the candles on the table reflected in his green-flecked amber eyes. They could have been beautiful if he hadn't been smirking in such a way that made me think he was trying to keep from laughing. I could swear he was biting the inside of his lip. This annoyed me as much as what Mother said. The death of a man wasn't something to laugh over. I also didn't like to be told I couldn't do something. My mother had never told me no when it came to my education.

Tesla wouldn't want anything to do with me, not in that way. He was a busy man. My mother's trepidation and Harrison's amused face were all it took for me to make up my mind. "The death was surely an accident, Mother." Of course, I would work in Tesla's lab. I'd even do a great job. "I think I'll do it. I'll work for Nikola Tesla," I said, resolution in my voice.

CHAPTER THREE

Mother sat in stony silence. There was no need to tell her of the scene I witnessed earlier. She was angry enough. The absence of sound stretched out until I couldn't bear it any longer.

"Actually," said Harrison, speaking up for the first time and breaking the spell. "Mr. Hill says those are only rumors, ma'am. It seems ladies fall for Mr. Tesla quite often, but he's too preoccupied with his work to pay them much mind."

I seized on my opportunity before Mother had a chance to say anything else. "See, dear? Mr. Tesla won't even know I'm there. It's all settled." I patted her hand as she had patted mine, turning my head in the direction of the first incoming course to avoid her narrowed eyes. The smell of roasting beef emanating from beyond the kitchen door set my mouth watering. The day had proved to be a long one. All I wanted was to eat and retire early.

The rest of the dinner was rather uneventful. Mr. Byrne and Mother spoke most of the time about various mundanities while my mind wandered to Mr. Tesla and his mysterious lab. What was it about him women fell in love with? I had never seen him myself. Dove, my best friend and neighbor, met him at a dinner not long after he arrived in town. According to her, he was tall and fit with dark, dreamy eyes. There was no doubt the man was a genius. He was renowned the world over for his electrical experiments. It was said that he never slept and rarely left his lab. Would I be able to keep up with him?

"Cora? Cora?" Mother's sharp voice snapped me from my reverie.

"Sorry, Mother, what did you say?"

"I said you must help me convince Mr. Byrne to stay the night. Conditions are quite treacherous outside."

I hoped my face didn't betray my annoyance at the thought of Mr. Byrne sleeping in our house. "I'm sure Mr. Byrne knows what's best for himself, Mother." I shifted in my seat. This meal couldn't end fast enough, so I could retire to my room. I wanted nothing more than to tuck myself into my warm bed and read by the soft candlelight, Willow by my side. After having been tight-laced into my corset for twelve hours, I was ready for some relief.

"I appreciate your concern, Mrs. Croft. If I could leave my buggy here until the roads are more passable, I should be fine—cold, but fine."

Mother could see she was beaten and did nothing to press her point. "Very well. You're a grown man. I can't force you to stay."

Mother's delicate hand reached for her crystal bell. When Phillips, the butler, appeared at her elbow, she said, "Phillips, please walk Mr. Byrne to the carriage house and see he gets safely on his way."

"Yes, ma'am." Phillips bowed his head and upper body, standing back for Mr. Byrne to rise from his seat and follow.

Mr. Byrne stood, folded his napkin, and set it next to his plate. He turned to Mother, taking her hand. "Thank you for your kindness and generosity, Mrs. Croft." He lightly kissed the tips of her fingers, causing me to wrinkle my nose. When Mr. Byrne looked toward me and caught my face scrunched up, he smiled. "Goodnight, Miss Croft." The devilish grin and sparkle in his eyes left me irritated and speechless.

All I could do was nod. Once the men departed the room, I was ready to make my escape. While Isabella took a sip of wine, I pushed my chair back from the table. This was the perfect moment to run.

"Just a moment, young lady." Mother still sat straight-backed in her chair, as though the discomfort of her clothing didn't bother her one bit. Perhaps after so many years of corseting, I, too, would be more comfortable and not in the current agony I found myself.

"What did you mean when you said the young man's death was surely an accident? Have you heard something at school?"

I resumed my seat, shoulders slumped forward. My mind raced with how to answer. How would Isabella feel about what I witnessed? She was behaving in such an overprotective way, I was nervous to say too much. When I could think of nothing to say but the truth, I spoke. "I came upon the scene late this morning, after leaving Mrs. Sutton's house."

Mother's eyes bulged from her head; her mouth set in a straight line. She at least had the breeding to know when to keep her mouth from gaping. She took a deep breath. "I see. When were you going to tell me this, Cora? It must have been awful for you."

I played with the beading of my gown, unable to meet my mother's eyes. "It was terrible. Much more so for that poor man. I'd rather not discuss it anymore, Mother. There was nothing to be done for him."

"Of course, dear. Did you see him fall?"

"Mother, please. I'm exhausted and must get into bed. We can talk more tomorrow." I leaned over to kiss her firm, warm cheek, then shuffled from the room with all the speed I could muster. What an odd question to ask. She was clearly as shocked as I was by the whole affair. This sort of death was unusual here, which was alarming for us all.

Walters hadn't told her, and for this I was grateful. If he

had, she would have been at the school to pull me out halfway through the day, and Mr. Hill may never have told me about Tesla.

My energy and spirits were low, the specter of the dead man floating in my mind. Walking on the soft carpet was no easier than walking through mud, exhaustion weighing down my limbs. The events of this long day were no doubt written in the creases of my face. If only I could wipe them away.

There were two rooms in the house I used as a refuge: the library and my bedroom. Opening the door to my private room felt like entering heaven. I sank into the velvet sitting cushion of a Queen Anne chair, the dusky purple my favorite color, and leaned forward to unlace my boots and kick them from my feet. My stockinged toes worked themselves into the fibers of the deep, plush carpet my mother brought from France, and some of the tension I felt melted away.

The door opened and in walked Marsh. "Let's get you out of that thing. I'm sure you're ready." I tried so hard to emulate Mother in her grace and poise but often felt as if I failed in to do so. My back was never as straight as hers, and I ate more than a lady should—my stomach often pressing uncomfortably in my stays. How I would love to give the contraption up altogether. Mother would be appalled. Dove would only laugh at me. She would say that no man would marry a lady without a tiny waist. "You can spread out later," she always explained.

Marsh unbuttoned the gown, lifting it off over my head. As she unlaced my corset, I inhaled and exhaled a huge gulp of delicious air. My first full breath of the day. My ribs ached from their confinement. I pressed my fingertips into the flesh of each bone, massaging them with a deep pressure.

"Better, love?" asked Marsh behind me.

"So much."

She patted me on the back and left me to finish the rest of my evening ablutions. I didn't need help with every little thing, preferring to do much of my dressing and undressing alone. I untied my bustle, letting it fall to the ground, and peeled off my corset the rest of the way. My shift was pulled off and into my nightgown I stepped.

Steam wafted from the hot water Marsh had left in the ewer. This I poured into the basin. I bent over, inhaling the lavender-scented steam. I dipped a cloth and proceeded to wash my face and neck. The warm water was heaven, soothing the trouble in my mind and warming me up from the outside in.

After toweling off, I removed the bed warmer Marsh placed between my covers. Slipping into cozy blankets felt like slipping into a dream. As I lay in bed, I thought about the day. I couldn't remember the last time so many events occurred so close together—a horrible death, an offer to work with Nikola Tesla, and a blizzard that would shut down the town for at least the next day or two.

I was in no way certain working with Mr. Tesla was the right choice. Would he accept me? Would I be able to keep up with his mind and handle his eccentricities? I didn't know the answer to any of these questions, but what I did know was I would try. The challenge was worth the uncertainty, and I would have stories to tell for ages.

The next day, we were snowed in. I felt some guilt not insisting Mr. Byrne stay the night but was sure he made it home safely. He seemed a capable enough man.

I lounged in my bath with the knowledge I had nowhere to rush off to this morning. There was no way to get out as it was. I hoped this wouldn't hurt my chances with Mr. Tesla. The man would understand. Unless he'd invented a way to do so, one couldn't control the weather.

I felt like a queen, luxuriating in the fragrant water. My fingers and toes, wrinkly like prunes, did nothing to speed me up. Small wisps of steam emanated from the surface of the water. I wrung out my cloth, draping the warm towelette over my face, and inhaled the rose scent of the bathwater. My mind drifted, my body relaxed.

A sharp knock on the door startled me, bathwater splashing over the side of the tub.

"Are you in there, Cora? It's after ten." Dove's musical voice sounded through the door.

"How on earth did you get here?" I asked, scrambling to grab at a towel. Dove lived next door, a mere fifty steps from porch to porch, but the drifts that had accumulated outside overnight were thigh deep.

"I wore Father's rubber boots and held up my skirts. I have a feeling I've scandalized the entire block. Hurry up and meet me in your room." The padding of feet receded down the carpeted hallway. Dove and I didn't stand on ceremony with each other. She was the one person with whom I ever felt comfortable being entirely myself.

I wrapped up in a blue velvet dressing gown and swept down the hall, the ends of my hair dripping wet. "Something must be important," I said as I crossed the room to hug my friend. Dove's face told me everything I needed to know.

She was happy, deliriously so. Her blue eyes shined, and her smile was as wide as I'd ever seen it. Although Dove was in stocking feet, her day dress of yellow silk trimmed in white lace was impeccable. Not a blonde hair on her head was out of place. This was Mother's ideal child: a girl who always looked put together and perfect. "Yes, Cora. Oh, it's so exciting. How could I wait for something as silly as the weather?" She sat in my chair, placing her gloved hands neatly in her lap. I noticed a small hole, the tip of her index finger visible through the worn threads. Never had I seen Dove with a hole or tear in any article of clothing. "He's gone to my father, Cora. He's asked for my hand," Dove practically squealed.

I kept my smile in place for her sake, not letting my disappointment show. "Mr. Sharp asked for your hand? So soon?"

Timothy Sharp, a wealthy businessman from Texas, currently resided at Glen Eyrie as a guest of General Palmer. This was only a temporary residence, as he made sure everyone was aware. Denver would be his permanent home, once he finalized his business here, that being railroads. As much as he enjoyed droning on about himself, he never made it too clear just what he had to do with the railroads. Mr. Sharp met Dove at The Opera House three weeks ago and began courting the next day. Three short weeks after, and here my friend was engaged.

"It isn't soon, Cora. Not when you know like Timothy and I do. I knew the second I saw him with that wicked glint in his eye as he watched me from his box. He's the perfect mix of gentleman and cad." Dove played with the buttons on her gloves.

"I'm so happy for you, really. I'm going to miss you, that's all. Home won't be the same without you next door." I sat on the bench at the end of my bed. My shoulders threatened to slump, but I did my best to keep my visage a happy one, plastering on a smile I didn't feel.

"I know. I feel it, too. But, Cora, Denver isn't so far away. And you can come and stay as often as you like, for as long as you like. Besides, you and I both know you won't be here forever. Your dreams will take you much farther away than Denver." Dove grinned, her cool eyes fixed on mine. "This time next year you'll be in New York or Boston, rubbing elbows with men from all over the world."

I couldn't help but laugh. Dove had been crazy for boys since she was twelve years old.

I wanted to be happy for my friend—I really did. All I could think about were the hundreds of times over the years we had run from one house to the other with stolen cookies from the kitchens in our pockets, climbing the trees out back until our palms bled, and sleepovers full of gossip and late-night laughter. Most importantly, the simple knowledge Dove was only a few steps away should I ever need her.

When my father's heart gave out unexpectedly, she slept on my settee for a week as I cried myself to sleep each night. What would I do without her now? I didn't like this change. I needed my friend.

"First thing will be the engagement party," continued Dove, not paying any mind to my fallen face. "General Palmer has offered to host the affair at Glen Eyrie. Exciting, isn't it?"

I forced a smile. "It is."

General Palmer was Dove's godfather. He doted on her as he did his own daughters. I wasn't surprised by the generosity. It was too bad the weather was already so cold—the grounds of Glen Eyrie were second to none in the city. An outdoor party with lanterns in all the trees would have been lovely.

"The house will be crammed full, but it will be marvelous. Of course, we'll have to have new gowns made. When can you go with me to the dressmakers? Tomorrow? The snow should be mostly cleared by then." Dove tilted her head, her bright blue eyes gazing at me expectantly.

"I'm not sure, my schedule may be changing. I haven't told you my news."

"Oh, Cora." Dove clapped her hands together. "I'm so sorry. Here I am being positively selfish. Tell me."

I shook my head, laughing. "Your news is more life-changing than mine." I paused, wondering if Dove would have the same reaction as Mother. "Well, I'm going to see about assisting Nikola Tesla in his lab. Mr. Hill thinks it will suit me. At least help me to gain some experience, something more for my applications." I shifted on the end of the bench, crossing my feet at the ankles under my dressing gown.

Her eyes went wide. "That is as thrilling as my news, Cora. An experimental lab is the perfect place for you. And, as I've said, Mr. Tesla is quite handsome. Strange, but handsome. You'll have to tell me more about him. He wasn't very forthcoming about himself at Mr. Priest's dinner. In fact, he seemed very put out to be there. He rolled his eyes several times and looked squeamish when Molly Parker twirled her hair at him."

Dove's reaction amused me. "Yes, I've heard the same. There's no guarantee he'll choose me, but I plan on trying. I think you're right. It is the perfect place; I can't wait to give it a go."

"You'll do wonderfully, and the man would be a fool not to take you on. Of course, he's the very opposite of a fool." Dove rose to her feet, the picture of elegance in every way. "I'll leave you to dress. It will take me the better part of an hour to re-mummify myself for the trek back. Don't forget about the gowns. We'll need to go soon. I can't wait any longer than the day after tomorrow. I'm thinking an icy blue silk with lily-white ruffles to match the snow."

"Blue is the perfect color for you. I'm sure you'll have a wonderful time choosing the gowns for the party and the wedding. No doubt Mr. Sharp will spare no expense for you." I meant the comment to be a light-hearted one. Instead, it sounded a little acidic.

Dove's eyes changed from bright and clear to narrowed and annoyed. "There are more reasons to marry than money, Cora. I would love Timothy even if he didn't have a dime to his name."

Sheepish, I bowed my head. "I'm so sorry. I only meant that all the planning will be such fun. I didn't mean to suggest otherwise."

"I know, Cora. Good luck with Mr. Tesla." Dove blew me a kiss and crossed to the door.

"I really am happy for you, dear," I lied to her back.

"So am I, Cora. So am I." She opened the door and was gone.

The snow was vexing. I had so much to do that being cooped up in the house made me anxious. my stomach was a little tight, and a pain had sprung up in the back of my neck. Pulling back the velvet curtains, I wiped off the accumulated condensation to peer out. I sighed with some relief. The only objects that fell from the sky were bright rays of sunshine. The giant flakes from the night before had ceased making their way to earth. Streams of light reflected off the banks of white snow, causing me to squint against the welcome assault.

Magpies streaked across the clear blue sky, not a cloud in sight. The snow was still deep, but I knew from a lifetime in the arms of the Rocky Mountains, the powder was already melting. If I could remain patient for this one day, by tomorrow I should be able to drive to Tesla's lab for my introduction.

Since I would be homebound for the remainder of the day, I didn't see why I should even bother to dress. Mother wouldn't approve if I remained in my dressing gown all day, though, so I rang for Marsh and chose a plain gray day dress with no embellishments. I hoped Mother wouldn't notice my corset-less figure. Laces would only impede as I bent over books and papers. Marsh twisted my hair into a simple bun, and I was ready for the library for a day of reading and drinking coffee.

As my foot hit the bottom stair, male laughter reached my ears. Laughter that sounded an awful lot like that of Harrison Byrne. The sound was a low, not unappealing, guffaw. Something bubbled uncomfortably in the pit of my stomach, my ears suddenly feeling hot. *I thought he went home.* Surely, he hadn't come back this morning. I crossed the hall as the clock struck eleven, chimes sounding down the hallway. The dark, bitter scent of coffee mingled with last night's roast beef. My mother, though wealthy, was also economical, and we often ate leftovers at luncheon.

"Cora, there you are. I wasn't sure if we would see you today." Mother was seated at the dining room table exactly as I had left her last night. I felt struck by déjà vu as my eyes fell on the face of Mr. Byrne. His amber eyes were crinkled at the corners by his caddish grin. Dove would have loved the mischievous way in which his mouth twitched.

"Is that Father's suit?" I blurted out, unable to stop myself. The navy-blue jacket was unmistakable, the lapels creased so they fell open wider than normal as Father preferred.

"Yes, dear. Mr. Byrne needed fresh clothes, and he is exactly your father's size. There's no sense letting good clothing go to rot."

I did everything in my power to hide my annoyance. Seeing Harrison Byrne in Father's suit jarred me. He'd been gone for years, yet his absence had remained fresh. The day we lost him was the worst day of my life.

"Sit down and join us for luncheon." Mother indicated my seat as I continued to stand awkwardly by the table. I pursed my lips and sat.

"I take it Mr. Byrne was unable to make it home last night." I snapped open my napkin, placing it in my lap. I looked at my mother and felt embarrassed. While Isabella was corseted and beautiful in a dark green silk dress, I was horribly drab by comparison. Had I known we had company, I would have made more of an attempt with my appearance. Even if it was just Harrison Byrne.

Mr. Byrne spoke, my gaze unable to meet his face. "I didn't make it ten feet. The snow was too deep by then for Rex to trudge through."

I was saved from further conversation by the serving of the midday meal, which gave the perfect excuse to turn away from the searching eyes of the man who sat across from me. My hopes of spending the day cozy in the library surrounded by books appeared to be in ruins.

"Whatever you were planning to do for the rest of the day, Cora, may now include Mr. Byrne. I have business to attend to in my study after we eat." Mother pierced a tiny piece of beef with her fork and placed it daintily in her mouth. She was telling me in no uncertain terms to step up and play hostess.

"Cora needn't bother to entertain me, Mrs. Croft. If

there's a book or two around, I'll have all the occupation I need."

Not only were my hopes dashed, but they were also destroyed. The morning had started with an off-putting encounter with Dove and now I was forced to entertain Harrison Byrne. I preferred to spend time in the library alone, even on days when I hadn't much to do. The library was my father's sanctuary. He and I had spent countless hours reading through his many books, laughing, and telling jokes. Father wanted more than anything that I should be as well educated as a son, while Mother insisted I also play the part of a lady.

I had rudely avoided Mr. Byrne's gaze long enough. Now I looked up into his eyes, mimicking my mother as best I could. "You are quite welcome to join me in the library, Mr. Byrne. My plans for the day revolve around reading and study, so it seems we could make amiable companions for the afternoon."

Mr. Byrne's smile widened. For the first time, I noticed his straight, white teeth. I caught my mother's eyes sliding toward me as she sipped from her teacup. No doubt my ladylike behavior had taken her aback.

After lunch, Mr. Byrne and I, chaperoned by a sleepy Willow, were settled in the library. It took him a few moments of muttering and perusing the long rows of books before choosing one with which to occupy himself. He chose Dickens' *A Tale of Two Cities*. A particular favorite of my father's.

"Have you read it?" He held up the worn leather copy and waved it in the air.

I situated a pillow behind me and nodded. "Yes, my father read it to me as a child. He loved that story. Father was equally fascinated and horrified by the French Revolution."

"I think I would've liked your father. He had good taste in books and furniture. This is a formidable room," he said as he situated himself into a deeply cushioned brown leather chair. "Very masculine," he added.

"Is that why you like it? The room meets your manly expectations?" I grinned at Harrison, who burst forth with another guffaw.

He propped a foot onto the ottoman. "I knew there was more personality in there than you let on." Harrison grinned back, but the comment annoyed me.

He could dangle his hook all he liked, I refused to take the bait. What I needed was for him to settle in and quiet down, not attempt to make conversation all day. I had studying to do if I were to speak intelligently to Mr. Tesla tomorrow. "Yes, well, this was my father's favorite room and the place he spent most of his time, so it reflects his taste. We read here together often," I said, not looking up, hoping he would take the hint.

Mr. Byrne wasn't wrong about the masculinity of the space. The room was paneled in rich mahogany, the kind men seemed to find so appealing. Bookcases, which matched the paneling, lined all four walls, save for the doorway and the bay window, where I currently sat. A dark burgundy, brocaded paper covered the bits of wall that peeked out here and there. Everything was a little severe. The one area of brightness and light came from the window that afforded a view of the south side of the property. From my seat, I could see Dove's home, Pikes Peak rising behind it.

There hadn't been much in the library that would help me with the sort of electrical experiments Mr. Tesla was performing. I pulled out all the scientific books I could find, feeling they were better than nothing. My pile mainly consisted of classics by Copernicus, Galileo, and Francis Bacon.

I looked out at the white-covered landscape, two books open in my lap. If the snow continued to melt throughout the day, by tomorrow afternoon, I would be able to ride to my destination with little trouble, as I'd previously thought.

"You seemed out of sorts at lunch, Cora. It's so much

more fun when you smile and lob jibes at me."

My back was to Mr. Byrne, and that was the way I preferred to keep it. Our moment of levity was amusing, but I had more pressing matters to tend to. "If you must know, my best friend is getting married and it's all a little sudden."

Harrison chuckled. "I see. Worried that you'll end up an old maid?"

I whipped my head around, upsetting the books in my lap. "How ridiculous. I wouldn't become any man's wife for all the riches in the world. I've no desire to marry, to be tied to someone for the rest of my life. I'm only worried for Dove. To run off with a railroad tycoon she barely knows is absurd."

"Who is she marrying, Timothy Sharp?" Mr. Byrne sat with his feet propped casually on the leather ottoman in front of him.

I nodded. "How do you know Mr. Sharp?"

"I cart him around quite a lot. Seems like a dandy, but you never really know. Just because he calls himself a railroad tycoon doesn't mean he *is* one. Lots of people say they're one thing when they're really something else."

I scrunched up my face. I doubted Mr. Byrne knew anything at all about Mr. Sharp, but I wanted to end the conversation and get to work, so instead of commenting, I re-opened a book.

An hour later, Mr. Byrne was fast asleep in his chair. I took my volumes up in my arms, motioned to Willow, and crept from the room. It wouldn't have been polite to disturb him, I told myself.

The rest of the day was spent on the floor of my bedroom, books spread all around. I really couldn't bear to sit through another meal with Mr. Byrne grinning at me all the way through. At dinner time, I sent Marsh down to tell Mother I had a headache and wished to retire early, excitement mounting for my adventure to the famous lab.

CHAPTER FOUR

The hallway was still dark as I walked on my tiptoes down its carpeted length. The sun had yet to rise and most of the house continued to sleep, including my mother. This was my chance to steal away before she could fix me in her disappointed stare. Mother was being irrational about Mr. Tesla, and I couldn't wait to prove her wrong.

I was practically dressed in another plain gray bustle gown underneath my winter coat. The hat perched to the side of my head was a simple ladies' carriage hat tied under my chin. Shielding my eyes from the glare of the sun off the white banks of snow would be imperative as the day wore on. The bright Colorado sun would rise high overhead. My attire did not say society girl, which was exactly what I wanted.

I crept into the kitchen, still freezing cold, the fire had yet to be lit, and pilfered two biscuits from the tin. This would suffice as my morning meal. These were wrapped in a napkin and slipped into my handbag. I was still inside and already shivering from the cold. The urge to go back to my warm bed to snuggle with my warm dog was almost overwhelming, but meeting with Tesla was more important than immediate comfort.

My heart was in my throat as I slunk through the house. It was silly to be so nervous in my own home. I didn't want to have to explain myself to anyone; I only wanted to get on my way.

"You're up early." I jumped at the voice of Harrison Byrne behind me. My shoulder slammed violently into the grandfather clock as I pitched forward; a gong echoing down the hallway.

With a scowl and narrowed eyes, I turned to face him, one hand massaging my wounded muscle. "Are you still here?" I whispered, venom dripping from my voice.

Harrison affected a casual devil-may-care attitude with his hands shoved in his pockets, his hat sitting almost sideways on his head. His eyes were bright and clear, a smile playing on his lips. Given the hour, his fresh appearance irritated me. "If you'll recall, I was unable to leave yesterday. I'm now on my way to the carriage house to saddle my horse and try for home. Where are you going?"

"I'm on my way to Mr. Tesla's lab. I understand he rarely sleeps, so he should be awake by the time I get there."

"Are you sure you're not trying to avoid your mother by sneaking out like a burglar before the sun is up?" Harrison's voice boomed down the small hallway, causing my stomach to constrict. His mouth widened into a full grin.

I dropped my hand from my shoulder to pull my gloves from my pocket. My eyes threatened to remain on his too long. "Can you please lower your voice? People are still asleep. I merely wanted to get a jump on the day."

With that, I turned on my heel, stalking my way to the back door. Somehow, Harrison Byrne made it there before me, his hand on the knob. He pulled the door wide.

"After you." He gestured for me to go ahead.

I tried to keep my eyes from narrowing but wasn't too successful. Outside on the graveled walk, I could see the snow, yesterday so deep, was already half melted. The main roads were sure to be cleared, at least mostly so, making my journey even easier.

"Watch out for ice," Mr. Byrne said behind me. A second later, there was a crunch of snow, a slap of flesh on the hard ground, and a yelp. "Ah!"

My eyes darted to the upstairs windows as I whirled around. The breath hitched in my throat; my gaze focused on my mother's closed curtains.

"Don't worry about me, I'll be fine."

I looked down at Mr. Byrne, clamping a hand over my mouth to keep from laughing out loud. He was flailing about like a turtle on its back. "I'm sorry. Are you hurt, Mr. Byrne?" Mindful of the icy path, I carefully scooted back to where he was lying, half-sprawled, off to the side of the path.

"Fine. I slipped is all. You should be familiar with the sensation." Mr. Byrne took hold of my free hand, then I pulled him to his feet.

"Very funny," I said dryly.

He took a moment to bend over, brushing the snow from his legs. "Cora, can you do me a favor and stop calling me Mr. Byrne? We've been schoolmates for a year now. It makes more sense for you to call me Harrison. I, for one, can't stand to always be so formal."

I looked at him for a moment. "I suppose it wouldn't hurt. It's not like I see you that often."

I smirked, turning to continue my walk down the path. The air was sharp, fresh. The cold, a slap in the face after the relative warmth of the hallway. The sky was beginning to lighten behind us. I knew the sun would soon rise to the east, opposite the dark outline of Pikes Peak I could see in the distance. The Peak was my favorite view, and I made it a point to look in its direction at least once a day. Even after all these years, I never tired of it.

The gently sloping mountaintop was covered in a thick layer of white snow. A stark contrast to the light dusting we began with yesterday. The arms of the Peak seemed to stretch out, sheltering Colorado Springs in the safety of its embrace.

I reached the side door of the carriage house well before Harrison, as I hadn't waited for him to catch up. I could hear him behind me, grunting with the effort of keeping his feet from slipping out from under him once again. The door proved to be a little stubborn, as a pile of snow had fallen from the eave and blocked the bottom. I tried to kick the wet snow with the toe of my boot, but it wouldn't budge.

"Frozen," I muttered to myself.

"Let me help you with that, Bird." It was a relief to hear the voice of Wolf, not Harrison Byrne.

I turned to smile at Marshall Ward, who worked odd jobs for us on occasion. Marshall was a few years older than me, although he appeared much older than that. His hair, a shaggy gray-brown, hung down over golden eyes that would have evoked fear in any other face. Since childhood, I'd called him Wolf, and he called me Bird. "Thank you. The snow has frozen solid, right underneath the door jamb."

"No problem," was all Wolf said as he bent down to handle the situation. Not known for his wordiness, Wolf was smart, capable, and very strong. Two solid whacks from his hand ax took care of the ice as it flew in all directions, landing on the carriage door and the hard ground, with the sound of a small explosion.

Harrison ambled up next to me, a little close, and muttered, "I could have done that."

I chose to ignore his comment and, instead, addressed Wolf. "What brings you here so early?"

Wolf straightened. He was slightly taller than Harrison, who I noticed was attempting to stand straighter. "I was working to clear some of the streets and thought I'd come over here to see how your walkways looked. Where are you off to?" Wolf eyed me suspiciously, then cast a gaze on Harrison.

"This is Harrison Byrne, a schoolmate. He's on his way, after having been stranded here. I'm off to Nikola Tesla's lab to see about his assistant's job."

Wolf's head snapped back to me. "You are? Do you

know Mr. Tesla?"

"I do not. Mr. Hill let me know he's looking for new help." I shrugged. "It doesn't hurt to give it a try."

Wolf nodded, looking down.

Just then, a thought occurred to me. "Wolf, you should come with me. Perhaps he could use us both."

I spoke quickly, without thinking. Wolf never attended school. His life had been a hard one, which forced him to work from a young age. Despite this, he was very knowledgeable in several subjects. Wolf and Father used to have long talks, and Father often lent him books to read, then discussed them with him at length.

Harrison bristled next to me. "I'm pretty sure he's only looking for one person."

"How would you know?" I unkindly snapped at Harrison before returning my attention to Wolf. "Come with me, Wolf, and we'll see what happens. Do you have the time?" I knew he would at the least love to meet Mr. Tesla.

"I do. If I'm ready by noon to accompany Anne Marie to her grandmother's, it shouldn't be a problem." Anne Marie was Wolf's fiancée. She was small and beautiful, like a fragile little doll. Next to Wolf, she appeared even smaller, but in a way that worked as a compliment.

"I don't see why it should." I ignored Harrison and strode into the carriage house. The temperature inside was a stark contrast to that of outside. It was warm, close, and pungent. The musky scent of the horses was, at first, always an assault to the senses.

Walters was beginning to stir in his room overhead; it was likely we woke him with the racket of trying the door. I felt so much time had already been wasted this morning. Now I would have to give another explanation as to where I was off to. When Wolf and Harrison walked toward the saddles, I went with them. Harrison reached for his saddle, Wolf for mine.

"I'll saddle my own horse. You can saddle Titan to ride,"

I said to Wolf, reaching for the saddle, which belonged to my grandmother once upon a time. The dark-brown leather gleamed from having been recently oiled.

"Let me help you, Bird. It's heavy." Wolf moved to take the saddle anyway, but I cut him off.

"I can manage. We need to get a move on."

Wolf shrugged. Relenting, he reached for another saddle.

Harrison snickered behind us. "Better let her do what she wants. She's going to do it anyway."

I sucked in a silent breath, brow knit in determination. I could do this. In one swift movement, I stooped over, gripped my saddle under the pommel and seat, and pulled it up toward my chest. I refused to grunt or make any other sound, knowing Harrison was watching me from the corner of his eye. I ground my teeth, shuffling toward my horse, the weight of the leather making my arms burn with the effort.

It was a triumph to make it alongside Lady. The hard part came next. My gaze darted from the saddle to the horse's slick, blonde back. There was no way I could sling the heavy bundle up and over the top of her. Perspiration gathered on my brow, the warmth of the carriage house and the burden in my arms conspiring against me.

"Let me get that for you, Miss." Walters's thick English accent was music to my ears. He materialized behind me, taking my burden out of my hands without so much as a sigh, and slung it with ease over my horse.

"Thank you, Walters," I said, trying not to breathe too deeply. I stood aside while Walters deftly went to his work, securing the saddle to Lady's strong, beautiful back.

Within minutes, the three of us were setting off down Wood Avenue in the direction of Mr. Tesla's lab. Harrison's buggy would remain in the carriage house until he was sure the roads were completely passable. Likely, one more day. If he tried to drive it along the roads too early, there was always the danger of losing a wheel in the thickness of the mud, then I'd never get rid of him.

The sun was rising on our left. Despite what promised to be a sunny day, our breath came out in big wafts of wispy air. The street was awakening. I could hear Dove's dog, Bitty, and his yappy bark as a servant let him out to use the yard. Birds were beginning to chirp, happy in the sunshine and melting snow.

The road was a sludge of mud and water, but not impassable by horse, and not slick with ice. Harrison was smart to leave the buggy. He trotted up alongside me, a little closer than what made me comfortable. His horse was bigger than Lady by two hands. The last thing I needed was for her to spook, throwing me into the mud. "You shouldn't have invited anyone else along. Mr. Tesla isn't looking for an army," he said crossly, his voice low.

I shot him a glance. "I don't think you're in any position to know Mr. Tesla's mind, Mr. Byrne. Why don't we let the man himself decide what he thinks is best?" I glanced back, but Wolf was several paces behind us, smoking a cigarette.

"We're back to Mr. Byrne now? I don't think I can read Tesla's mind. I just don't want anyone to stand in the way of you getting the job." Harrison snapped his reins and trotted ahead, his horse flinging sludge onto the legs of mine.

I shook my head and looked away. What was it to Harrison Byrne, anyway? Why should he care if I worked at the lab or didn't? I couldn't make any sense of the man.

I didn't have to think on Harrison for long. The sight of the college up ahead drew my attention. I glanced from Cutler Hall over to the brick of Coburn Library.

As we approached the library, a small man stood on the side of the road, his hand raised in hello. Maxwell Priest was round of figure with small, dark eyes that one could describe as beady. He smiled crookedly as he waved me over. Mr. Priest taught science at the college, his old East Coast money keeping him in one fresh suit after the next. He was a would-be scientist, having at one time worked as an assistant to Thomas Edison at Menlo Park.

"Cora Croft. What are you doing out and about on such a cold day, and so early?"

I pulled Lady to a stop alongside Mr. Priest as he reached out to pat her head.

"Wolf and I are going to the experimental station to speak with Mr. Tesla. According to Mr. Hill, he's looking for an assistant." I spoke down to Mr. Priest from the saddle. It was probably rude of me not to dismount, but I was tired of all the delays. At this rate, I would never meet the man of the hour.

Maxwell Priest took a step back, his gaze trained on mine. He seemed to be deep in thought for a moment as his eyes glazed over, and he appeared to chew on the inside of his lip. "How interesting," he finally said. "Well, Miss Croft, if you find yourself with the job and feel you are out of your element, I'm always here to help. It would interest me a great deal to learn more of what goes on out there." His stare left my face, darting around the street.

My grip tightened on the pommel of the saddle. I took a deep breath, trying not to betray my feelings. "Thank you, Mr. Priest. I'll keep that in mind," I said this with much difficulty. "Now, we must be off before we lose any more of the day. Good morning." I inclined my head, moving Lady onward.

Harrison and Wolf waited for me not far ahead. Harrison leaned to the side. "What was that about?"

I sighed, pulling a face. "He offered to help me should I have any questions about the work at the lab."

Wolf smiled, looking toward the mountains so I couldn't see him. Harrison had less tact and laughed out loud. "I'm surprised you didn't kick him," Harrison said between snorts.

I moved Lady into a trot, heedless to the mud. Separating myself from Harrison Byrne was all I cared about. The sun was inching higher to our left, the orange and red bursts of color from the sunrise enhanced by the blanket of white on the earth. I tried to focus on the beauty of the morning, not my irritation with Harrison. Although cold, the sun was warm, my exposed skin losing a measure of frigidity. The day promised to be a lovely one.

Ten minutes later, with my stomach about to rumble, my companions and I neared Harrison's neighborhood. He had taken the lead, riding ahead of us the rest of the way in blissful silence.

"Well, I guess this is where we leave you," I called to his back as I drew the two biscuits from my handbag. I offered one to Wolf, who rode alongside me.

Harrison pulled up on his reins, bringing Rex to a stop. Wolf and I moved next to him. Harrison turned in his saddle, a wide grin on his face. "Afraid not. Mr. Tesla will be expecting me."

My mouth dropped open, crumbs from the biscuit falling down my chest. "What do you mean?" I asked with a full mouth.

Wolf chuckled on his horse. He sat, regarding us both, as he ate his biscuit, a twinkle in his eye I didn't care for. If I were less of a lady, I would have stuck out my tongue at the pair of them.

"I mean what I said. Mr. Tesla, my employer, will be expecting me." Harrison clucked his tongue at Rex, who continued moving along.

I clamped my mouth shut, urging Lady forward. "Wait one minute." My voice was louder than I intended. I swallowed the dry biscuit with some effort, almost choking on the food and my anger. "You work for Tesla? As an assistant?"

Harrison looked over his shoulder, a smug look on his face. "In the mornings, three days a week before school. Mr. Hill thought it best I keep the job to myself or else I'd be swamped with questions. I'll be happy to make the introductions." He looked forward.

My ears and cheeks felt hot, and not from frostbite. I fumed. He deliberately kept this from me to reveal at what he thought would be the perfect moment. Not only was this irritating, but the thought of working alongside Harrison Byrne in what were, no doubt, close quarters was intolerable. I had half a mind to turn around and go back home.

That was until I saw the lab before me.

All the annoyance washed away. The building wasn't terribly interesting, but there was something here, something exciting.

The outside of the lab was plain enough, seemingly nothing more than a large barn. It was the tall wooden tower on top that caught my attention. I knew from the talk at school that it was eighty feet high. The tip could be seen from school, but seeing it up close was astounding.

Even more intriguing was what looked like a copper ball erected over the roof by a pole longer than the tower. The copper glinted in the sunlight like a beacon. We walked the horses through a high fence. Signs everywhere read *Keep Out—Great Danger.*

My instinct was to turn around and flee. My stomach did a flip-flop, my pulse picking up speed. But as Harrison kept going, so did I. A good distance from the lab, he finally stopped, dismounting from Rex and tying him to a pole next to a small trough. I followed suit, handing him my reins, Wolf right behind me. I walked around Lady, my eyes taking in the sight.

Movement in the doorway startled me. A man's head peered out from the open door.

"Harrison, where have you been?" the accented voice called out.

Harrison moved next to me, placing his hand under my elbow. "Get ready to meet Mr. Tesla."

CHAPTER FIVE

If my stomach was flipping before, now it threatened to drop completely. I was suddenly nauseated. Nikola Tesla stepped out from behind the wall, emerging fully in the doorway. He was as Dove described, tall and lithe of figure with a shock of dark hair and a thick, dark mustache. He wore a white shirt underneath a gray vest, gray pants, and a black tie studded with a diamond tie pin, which winked in the light. I couldn't tell from our distance of about thirty feet if he was smiling or scowling. Even minus a jacket, he appeared more dressed for dinner than work in a lab.

The sun was fully rising from behind the building. The light glared off the copper so bright I had to squint my eyes. Harrison trotted ahead of Wolf and me, meeting Tesla as he ambled down the three wooden steps. I could feel Wolf watching me, but feared if I looked at him, I would lose my nerve.

"Sorry, sir." I heard Harrison say. "I was snowed in over at Miss Croft's house. Mr. Hill over at the school told her you were considering a new assistant."

"But there are two of them." Tesla stared, hands on his hips, from me to Wolf then back at Harrison.

I cleared my throat and spoke up. "I brought Wolf,

thinking perhaps you could use us both, sir."

Tesla seemed to ponder this a moment as he stared into my eyes. I tried to keep myself from squirming under his scrutiny by shoving my hands into my pockets to fidget with the material. He stood impassively, his gaze never leaving me. I wondered how long we would have to stand like that before he spoke.

Wolf and I moved alongside Harrison; a ring of schoolchildren gathered around their teacher. If only he would speak and break the spell.

"Miss Croft, was it? Have you ever worked in an experimental lab before?"

I wanted to laugh at the absurdity of the question. There weren't many labs like his in the country, let alone the state.

Harrison continued before I could speak a single word. "Whether she has or not, she's the smartest in our year. Cora will surely be heading to a university in the Fall, any university she chooses."

I pursed my lips, sliding my eyes toward Harrison. He made me look weak in front of Mr. Tesla, whether he realized it or not. "I didn't need you to speak for me, Mr. Byrne."

My attention returned to Mr. Tesla. "I haven't worked in a lab like yours; however, I earned first prize in last year's science fair with my experiment on phototropism. I'm also a quick learner, a hard worker, and I'm truly fascinated by what you've accomplished. Your triumph in Chicago, at the World's Fair, was incredible." Suddenly, I wanted to work here more than anything in my life, but I was beginning to feel as though I was ill-prepared for any questions he may have for me.

Tesla's eyes slid to Wolf. "And you?"

"I've no formal training, sir. I'm inquisitive and capable. I'm at your disposal if you can use me, even if it's just to dig trenches. Honestly, it's just an honor to meet you." Wolf stuck out his hand, his golden gaze fixed on Tesla's dark one.

Tesla's eyes crinkled ever so slightly at the corners as he shook Wolf's hand. "Who needs formal training? In my experience, an inquisitive mind and a solid work ethic are all one needs to succeed." He paused, tapping his hip with a finger. "I'm nearly halfway finished here and could use the hands. You will have to sign a paper saying you'll preserve the confidentiality of my work with no exceptions. Many of my ideas have been stolen. If I find you have taken something off-premises or spoken of my experiments to anyone, you will be terminated and possibly sued. Are we clear?"

Wolf and I agreed. I felt elated we would be allowed entry into what I was sure was a magical place. Lewis Carroll's Wonderland came immediately to mind. Tesla continued to watch us for a moment longer. I grew increasingly uncomfortable under his gaze, feeling quite warm even though the temperature wasn't above thirty degrees.

"All right then, I can't stand here all day, and I've had such ill luck since arriving that I don't have the time to vet the two of you any further. Just know, if you fail to complete even the simplest task, you will be dismissed without discussion. Mr. Hill seems to know what he is about, so I will have to trust his recommendation of you, Miss Croft, and, summarily, your recommendation of your friend. Here's my list, Harrison. Please be quick about acquiring the items. I've lost a whole day to this blasted snow." Tesla held out a piece of paper, dug from his pocket. Harrison took it, slipping the paper into his own.

"You're not going to work in the lab?" I asked him.

"I'm not a lab assistant. I'm more of an errand boy."

Tesla chuckled. "All work has merit. You two with me."

For the first time in two days, I felt distressed by the thought of Harrison leaving. Two hours earlier, I couldn't wait to be rid of him. Now I longed for the familiarity. At least I had Wolf with me. The decision to bring him along seemed all the better. I took a deep breath, following Tesla up the stairs into the cavernous space of the lab.

Wolf and I stood at the threshold side by side. My head turned every which way as I took it all in. The main part of the room was laid out in a circular pattern, surrounded by a kind of waist-high fencing. A cylindrical oscillator stood in the center with several coils grouped together next to it. I knew what this was, as I had read about it in the local paper. There was a hot, sharp odor in the air that reminded me of burning metal. This was surely from the electrical charges given off during experiments. I buzzed with excitement. Wonderland, indeed.

"Over here, please," Tesla called to us from the far side of the room.

I could see a small door, which he now walked through. We followed.

The anteroom in which we stood housed a large sink, a couple of tables, and various tools of all kinds. Crates stacked in the corner looked as if they may topple over at any moment. The room was small, packed with all manner of items. He must need these things out of the way as he conducted important experiments in the main room.

Tesla handed a stack of papers toward me. "You will type these and send them to my assistant in New York. You"—he indicated Wolf—"will sit here and catalog these plugs. There is a notebook." Tesla pointed to the table covered with electrical items.

I looked down at the papers in my hands, my heart sinking. "You want me to type?" My hand started to shake. I was afraid my temper would get the better of me. "Because I'm a woman?" I blurted.

Tesla looked at me blankly. "Are you a woman? I hadn't noticed. Here." He took the papers from me and handed them to Wolf. "You type—you sort. It makes no difference to me as long as the tasks are completed. I have other work to do and can't be bothered with mundanities. This brings me to an important point, which I thank you for bringing up, Miss Croft."

Tesla looked at my ears, then seemed to gaze at my hair. I involuntarily raised a hand to my hat, pulling it down farther.

"A couple more things. I can't abide earrings. Please refrain from wearing any, Miss Croft. Also, I'm not fond of hair. Please always keep yours up and out of the way. That goes for you, as well, Mr. Wolf." Tesla moved his scrutinizing gaze to Wolf, who pulled a leather band from his pocket. Wolf pulled his foppish hair back and tied it up in the band. Tesla nodded his approval.

With that, Tesla turned abruptly, leaving us alone in the small room.

"Great," Wolf groaned. "I've never typed anything in my life."

I grunted. "Oh, give it to me." I snatched the papers from his hand before plopping into a rickety wooden chair that creaked beneath my weight. This table held nothing but a typewriter and a half-used pencil.

The room smelled like oil and rust, but at least it was warm. I had that to be thankful for.

Wolf grinned as he sat at the other table. "Thanks, Bird. What do you make of him so far?"

Truthfully, I felt disappointment but wasn't ready to voice this. "I'm sure it will get better. Science isn't only exciting experiments. There's a lot of preparation and planning. Calculations need to be made, materials gathered. We'll get to do something fun at some point. I'm sure of it." I said this more to convince myself than anyone else as I jammed fresh paper into the typewriter moments before I began banging on the keys.

I was slow with the machine. Never had I used one before. Deciphering Tesla's words wasn't any easier than learning where the keys were. His scrawl was like that of a child or a man without the time to write out his words with care. At this rate, it would take me hours to finish the simple task. Maybe by then we would have something more interesting to do.

The papers were twenty-seven pages of calculations and findings. From what I could follow, Tesla was conducting wireless telegraphy from Pikes Peak to Paris. He had produced artificial lightning, investigated atmospheric electricity, and was in the middle of proving the earth was a conductor. The man had been busy. No wonder he didn't have time to sleep.

The last two pages were the oddest. I read and re-read them to make sure I understood. Mr. Tesla had observed signals from space he believed were from extraterrestrials. The signals were repetitive, different from anything he'd ever observed on earth. He concluded the notes with a drawing for a new telescope he believed he could use to communicate with other planets. I had to bite my tongue to keep from blurting this out to Wolf. We weren't supposed to talk of what we learned here, even with each other.

What must have been two or three hours later, I typed the final word of the last page. My stomach growled audibly. I let out a deep breath, slouching into the back of the hard chair. My body sore from shoulders to thighs. "That was horrible," I whispered to Wolf.

His task had finished long ago. He now sat opposite me, organizing the papers into a neat pile as I finished typing them.

"What do you think he'll have us do now?" Wolf asked as he straightened all the papers together.

"I don't know. He hasn't checked on us once."

If Tesla wouldn't come to us, I would go to him. To sit and wait was not my style. As I rose from the table, Tesla's voice boomed out. "Nobody move!"

Wolf's hands flew to his mouth. Beyond the open door, lightning crackled and flashed across the room in a great cacophony of sound and light. The hairs on my arms and head stood at attention. I froze, half-stooped, my hands on the top of the table to support my weight. I was afraid to sit back down.

Wolf's eyes were wide. Strands of his hair had been

pulled out of his band, standing straight up all over his head. His hands dropped from his mouth.

"Wonderful, wonderful." From the corner of my eye, still frozen in place, I watched as Tesla walked toward the anteroom, scribbling in a notebook as he did so. He stopped, surveyed the room, and nodded. "Excellent. You may both leave. I'll need you back at the same time tomorrow." He didn't once look at either of us. He spun around, continuing to scribble as he went back to his chair near the oscillator.

Wolf and I exchanged a look. "That's all?" I mouthed, not wanting Tesla to hear me complaining.

My shoulders slumped as we marched by Mr. Tesla toward the front door. Wolf said goodbye as we left, Tesla never acknowledging that he heard. I was already too terrified of the man to tell him I had classes in the morning. I would have to speak with Mr. Hill.

Wolf and I mounted our horses. My stomach growled again, so loudly that I was embarrassed. It would have to wait. I told Wolf to head home without me. I had a stop to make.

Although there was still a good deal of snow on the ground, the roads were now mostly clear, the afternoon not too cold. The fresh air was pleasant after the closeness of the small anteroom with its mechanical odors. The clean sharpness of the melting snow cleared my senses.

The Rocky Mountains were a beautiful deep blue underneath the bright white tops of the peaks, the sun shining overhead. I made it to Mr. Hill's house without a problem, hoping to catch him home for lunch. I dismounted Lady, leaving her tied to a pole outside the neat clapboard cottage. The green boards, trimmed in scalloped white, reminded me of a sweet gingerbread house.

Mrs. Hill met me at the door, wiping her hands on her crisp white apron, her smile wide and warm. "Well, Cora. I haven't seen you in ages. What a lovely surprise."

I returned her smile as I moved onto the porch. "It's nice

to see you, Mrs. Hill. I hope I'm not interrupting, but I hoped to catch Mr. Hill before he returned to the school for afternoon classes."

Mrs. Hill held the door open wider. "He's just sitting down. I'll set a place for you to join us if you like."

My stomach growled again. My hands flew over my belly, as if I could help quiet it down. Mrs. Hill stifled a laugh with the back of her hand.

"Yes, please," I said, my cheeks burning.

The aromas from the dining room set my mouth to watering as soon as I walked in. Slices of fresh ham along with butter and rolls graced the table. Mr. Hill sat at the head in his shirt sleeves with his collar unbuttoned.

"Cora," he began, rising from his seat. His hands flew to his collar.

"Please, remain comfortable, Mr. Hill. I apologize for dropping in on you this way. I need to talk with you, if you don't mind, and Mrs. Hill invited me to stay for luncheon."

Mr. Hill nodded, then stepped forward to pull out the chair to his left. "You're welcome anytime. Please sit."

Mrs. Hill was at my elbow, placing a setting for me on the table with a practiced hand.

"Thank you, so much," I said to both as soon as we were all settled.

Mr. Hill served the ham as his wife passed me a roll. "This is wonderful," I said between mouthfuls. After a big gulp of lemonade, I continued. "I went to Mr. Tesla's lab this morning."

Mr. Hill perked up. "Did you? What do you think?"

"I'm not really sure what to think. I didn't much want to go. When I decided I would, I was excited to meet him and see his marvelous creations. But, when I arrived, he gave me such a menial task—typing, of all things. The one exciting moment came at the end with electricity flashing all around the main room beyond. I couldn't see much, and it was over so quickly. Then, he was ushering us out."

"Us?" inquired Mr. Hill.

"Yes, I brought along Marshall. You know Marshall, Mr. Hill."

Mr. Hill nodded. "I understand your disappointment, Cora. You were expecting to be involved in his experiments right away. To a man like Mr. Tesla, no task in his lab is a trivial one. Everything has a purpose. He uses his time fully and purposefully. Perhaps you should look at the task he set you in a different light. He allowed you a glimpse into his mind. He allowed you to see his written words, no matter the content."

I looked down at my plate as I listened to Mr. Hill speak. He was right. The notes I typed were personal notes and correspondence. Mr. Tesla said he had been stolen from in the past, yet he allowed me to see what were, no doubt, confidential records. Before I could respond, Mr. Hill continued.

"Don't forget, Cora. Every part of the scientific process is important. It all leads to something."

I shifted in my seat, feeling a little foolish for complaining. "You're right. It's an honor to be there, helping him in any way I can."

"It truly is. He's discovered so much already."

We continued to eat. I told Mr. Hill I would miss the next day's classes.

"I figured as much. Work at the lab whenever he needs you. You're so far ahead this year as it is, a few weeks of missed classes won't matter, and we can use your experience as credit. And with fall break coming up, you'll have plenty of time."

I left Mr. Hill's home grateful for the attention he was willing to give his students. After our discussion, my mind was re-focused on the task at hand. The interesting stuff would come with time. Right now, I was willing to help Mr. Tesla with every menial task he wished to hand me. Perhaps I'd even find out more about the poor man I saw on the flagstones and what exactly he did for Nikola Tesla.

CHAPTER SIX

The warm comfort of my room was everything I needed after the sparseness of the anteroom and the waning evening temperature. Dancing multi-colored light filtered in through the large stained-glass mural set atop the window framing my reading seat. I often dragged one of my grandmother's handmade patchwork quilts to this alcove along with a book to while away a lazy afternoon. With all that was happening, I wasn't likely to have one of those for a while.

At the very least, I was looking forward to a hot bath of sudsy bubbles to scrub away the metallic smell I felt was permeating my skin and hair.

But peace was not to be had, as Mother barged in right as I was preparing my toilette. "Sneaking out like a thief in the middle of the night, Cora? How unbecoming." Mother's face was cool, stony. It was her eyes that blazed with fury. "I told you I didn't want you working in that lab. Anything but that."

"Why are you so set against this?" I expected her to be irritated with my actions. I did not expect her to be angry, as she was generally so supportive. My cheeks warmed, then I realized my own temper must be held in check, were I to get my way in this.

Mother stood rigidly in front of me, a shadow passing behind her eyes. "I have my reasons."

I knew from experience; this was the most I could expect by way of an explanation. I clasped my hands in front of me like a penitent child, employing the most contrite expression I could manage, eyes like a puppy, mouth on its way toward pouty. "I apologize, Mother. Really, I do. I know I went against your wishes. The fact is the experience I could gain from working with Mr. Tesla could be invaluable for my future. If this goes well, I could have my pick of universities. You know as well as I do the battle I face as a woman seeking higher education. Mr. Tesla clearly doesn't see things like gender. Imagine if he wrote me a recommendation. I could go anywhere I pleased. Besides, Wolf is also helping at the lab, so I'm not alone with anyone." I sat on the end of my bed, gripping the corner post as I spoke for added emphasis.

I hadn't expected to say what I did about the recommendation. Once I verbalized these thoughts, I knew the truth of them. If Tesla liked me, if he found me clever and useful, perhaps he would give me a letter. As varied as his success had been, a recommendation from him would open doors all over the world.

Mother seemed to consider what I said. Her face softened as she looked down at her hands. "I suppose you're right, Cora. Although I don't love the thought of you out there surrounded by men, I have to admit you have a point." She looked back into my eyes. "Please be careful. You're still my little girl, whether you like it or not. There's no reason for you to get too close to Mr. Tesla." Isabella swept to the door then turned back to me. "I almost forgot to tell you, Maxwell Priest will be joining us for dinner this evening." She slipped out, leaving me with my thoughts, which now, annoyingly, included Maxwell Priest.

It seemed a bit of a coincidence that Mr. Priest would be coming for dinner the very same day I spoke with him about

Tesla's experimental station. No doubt he wished to ask me all manner of questions. Won't he be disappointed to learn all I did was type a fistful of notes? Since I was bound by confidentiality, I couldn't talk of what I had read, anyway. Maybe I would be cheeky and make something up.

Mr. Priest, in a perfect black suit with a single hothouse rose tucked into his lapel, stood as I walked into the parlor. The room was Mother's favorite, all floral patterns and brocades. Her portrait, painted by a French artist when she was twenty years old, hung over the fireplace. The gown she wore for the painting was daring for the time. Gauzy, low-cut white silk fell off her shoulders, revealing so much pale skin, little was left to the imagination. The portrait, which scandalized her parents, was my father's favorite piece of personal art. He often said Mother looked like a Greek goddess, not a mortal like the rest of us. Tonight, she appeared no less immortal in a purple silk gown that accented her curves and youthful appearance.

"Miss Croft, twice in one day, how fortuitous. How charming you look in blue. It won't be long before you're fielding offers of marriage, Isabella, if you're not already." He reached for my hand, bowing over it with formal grace.

"Thank you, Mr. Priest. How was your class on this cold, snowy morning?" I sat across from Mr. Priest, alongside my mother on the burgundy brocade divan.

Mr. Priest crossed his legs, waving his hand. "Oh, the same as always. There isn't much excitement to teaching. The excitement is in the experimentation. Tell us, how was your day with Mr. Tesla?"

It hadn't even taken five minutes before Mr. Priest was asking me about the lab. I folded my hands in my lap, blinking my lashes like I'd no idea what he was after. "About as uneventful as yours, it seems. There really isn't anything to talk of."

Mr. Priest laughed. Sinking back into the cushions of the

settee, he fixed me in his narrowed gaze. He was trying at playfulness and failing. "Come now, my dear. I know from personal experience that Nikola Tesla does not waste his time or anyone else's. He had you engaged in some task, I'm sure."

A muscle in my neck twitched, my smile faltering for a moment. "I assure you, Mr. Priest, all I did was type a correspondence to a friend in New York. Boring chit-chat is all I was privy to today."

Mr. Priest's eyes seemed to narrow further. Was he angry?

Mother chuckled next to me, patting my hand. "If that's all you'll be doing, I doubt you'll last long. You should be challenged by more than letters between friends, Cora."

The German clock on the mantel struck eight, interrupting our conversation for the present. Isabella rose to go to the dining room, and I followed, my eyes trained on the ground as I rose, so as not to look at Mr. Priest.

The table was set for the first course as we seated ourselves, Mother at the head, me in my usual spot to her left, and Mr. Priest in the chair across from me, generally reserved for guests. Once napkins were placed on our laps and the three of us were left to begin, I feared Mr. Priest would dive back in. Instead, he took a different tack.

"Isabella, you knew the gentleman who died so unfortunately, didn't you?"

I was so shocked by this question, my head snapped toward my mother, my spoon halted in mid-air, drops of creamy soup plopping back into the bowl. She took the question in stride, as she did most things. A surprise attack against my mother was not easily made.

"I did. This is a small city, Maxwell. I know many of its inhabitants. I'm sure you knew him, as well, being that he worked for Mr. Tesla and attended the college." Mother sipped her soup with more elegance than the queen.

I tried not to laugh as I looked down at my bowl. It seemed Mr. Priest had hoped to catch Mother in something, and, instead, she lobbed the question right back.

"Of course, I did. The young man, Joe Williams was his name, took several classes from me over the last two years. It's a shame what happened." Mr. Priest leaned over his bowl, taking a loud slurp from his spoon.

Phillips, the butler, appeared silently at Mother's elbow. "Mrs. Mackenzie is here to see you, ma'am. She says she only needs you for a moment and doesn't want to disturb the whole table. Some wedding business, I believe."

Mother daintily dabbed the corners of her mouth, folded her napkin, and pushed back her chair. Mr. Priest rose alongside.

"Please excuse me," she said to no one in particular, then swished from the room.

I resumed eating, feeling awkward at being left alone with Mr. Priest. After a few minutes of silence, I looked up to see him watching me as I ate. My skin crawled.

He smirked, a look of arrogance on his face I had never seen before. "You should ask your mother more about her relationship with Joe Williams," he said, his lids half-closed, his voice low.

Something made me lean forward, when in actuality, what I wanted to do was move as far away from him as possible. "Why would I do that, Mr. Priest?" I genuinely wanted to know. The look in Mr. Priest's eye was very strange. What was going on here?

Mr. Priest opened his mouth to respond as Mother swept back into the room. His jaw snapped shut as he looked away. Whatever he wanted me to know was secretive enough that he couldn't speak in front of Mother. My gaze darted back toward my bowl. She wouldn't keep a social relationship secret. Unless there was something about the relationship that must be kept confidential. I shook my head.

Ridiculous.

"Forgive me," she said as she sat back in her place. "Mrs. Mackenzie wants my help with the flowers for Dove's wedding. The affair is to be quite grand, Cora. We'll have to employ some more hands to help us."

One of my mother's many talents was a skill for flower arranging. Dove's wouldn't be the first wedding she assisted with. Mother had a keen eye for aesthetic beauty of all kinds.

The conversation turned to the city's recent structure fires. The Broadmoor Casino burned down two years ago and was quickly rebuilt. The Antler's Hotel, which burned almost exactly one year ago, was now being reconstructed. I couldn't have been less interested. My mind wandered throughout the remaining courses. I kept thinking about what Mr. Priest had suggested.

What could Mother possibly know about Joe Williams?

I didn't have the chance to ask her before turning in. Mother stayed up to play cards with Mr. Priest, and I couldn't keep myself awake. This would require further investigation.

The next morning, I strode up to the lab determined to do whatever Mr. Tesla asked of me, no matter how inconsequential it seemed. I dressed even more plainly than the day before—no ornamentation, no hat, no bustle, nothing which could interfere with my movement or catch a spark from the light show. I was careful to pin my hair back, so not a single strand was in danger of falling out. However strange I thought Mr. Tesla's statement on hair and earrings had been, I would not give him any reason to be uncomfortable.

The air was still cold, although not as bitingly. The sun was shining, rising in the east. I turned my face toward the warmth, closing my eyes for a moment to allow the rays to bathe me in their light. The day was full of possibilities.

"Are you in mourning, Cora?" Harrison's voice startled my eyes open. He poked his head out of the door in the same manner Tesla had yesterday.

I smoothed down the front of my black crepe gown,

proudly. "Stop being ridiculous. I only want to blend in."

"Not sure how you're going to manage that." Harrison winked.

An unwitting bloom of heat ignited my cheeks in the crisp morning air. I chose to ignore the remark, bounding up the steps and walking right past him without stopping.

"You may want to wait a second," Harrison said to my back.

Before I could ask why, I heard Tesla yell, "Please leave!"

My gaze darted around the space, fearful he was speaking to me. Had I done something wrong? Typed his papers incorrectly? Tesla was nowhere to be seen. I felt frozen to my spot, unsure of what to do. A moment later, the man himself came striding out of the anteroom. He stood aside, gesturing with his arm as he pointed to the main doorway. Tesla was frantic, his face glowing red as beads of sweat slid down his temples. He was looking back into the room at someone I couldn't see.

I stepped back alongside Harrison. "Who is in there?" I whispered. My stomach constricted as I thought he could be talking to Wolf.

"I don't know. Just got here and thought it best to hold back a sec." Harrison spoke in hushed tones under his breath. He looked fresh as always in his neat brown suit, hands rakishly askew in his pockets. There was no one who could pull off casual nonchalance like Harrison Byrne.

As I watched the scene before me, the object of Tesla's ire finally emerged from the small room beyond. I sucked in a hard breath, my mouth falling open before I could help it. The man who now faced Tesla's consternation with a blindingly bright smile on his lips was Timothy Sharp, the fiancé of my best friend.

Mr. Sharp's gaze drifted past Tesla and fell on me. I pressed myself against the wall, hoping to make my form less noticeable.

Please don't address me.

I held my breath.

Despite the quick prayer I offered up, he bellowed, "Cora Croft. What on earth are you doing here?" Timothy Sharp walked past Tesla on long, strong legs, his perfect camel wool coat billowing out as he did so. Mr. Sharp was a bit of a dandy, as Harrison had said, more so than Mr. Tesla and Mr. Priest combined. He wore the finest clothes, black hair perfectly pomaded, silver-tipped cane in one hand, black top hat casually dangling in the other.

Tesla followed Timothy; his eyes narrowed. "You know this man, Miss Croft?" His voice was sharp, clipped.

"Y-yes, sir, a little," I stammered. "Mr. Sharp is engaged to my friend, Dove Mackenzie."

There was no point in lying. If Mr. Tesla wanted to throw me out, there was nothing I could do about it. Moisture began to break out along my hairline. Would Timothy Sharp knock down all the pins I was struggling to keep in place?

Mr. Sharp nodded, winked at me, and then turned back around, almost bumping into Tesla, who came fast behind him. "Don't worry, old chap. Don't take anything out on poor Cora; she barely knows me." He popped his hat on his head in one liquid movement. "I'll be going now. Good day, Nikola."

Tesla's face was purple, his eyes bloodshot, fists clenched at his sides. Timothy Sharp turned in his expensive shoes, bowing toward me before exiting the building. Harrison and I stood mute as we waited for the hammer to fall.

The second Timothy crossed the threshold and was gone, Tesla let out a long breath, his body shaking with the effort of the exhalation. He raked his hands through thick, brown hair. "That man was snooping. How did he get in here?" Tesla looked from Harrison to me.

Harrison moved a step further into the room. "Cora only just arrived, and I've been here about two minutes longer. I'm sorry, sir, but the door was wide open."

Tesla regarded Harrison through narrowed eyes. "I

suppose it was my fault leaving it open. I needed the air." He shoved his hands into the pockets of his trousers. "I know that man. He's friends with that would-be scientist, Maxwell something, who imagines himself friends with Edison. Our world is a small one." He walked in a small circle, chin cupped in his hands. Tesla's eyes were the only thing that betrayed his lack of sleep. His hair, tousled though it was, was neat and clean. His clothing—a pristine white shirt underneath a black, pinstriped vest over matching pinstriped slacks—all freshly pressed. "I need to regroup, create a plan for the day. Find something to do." Tesla waved us away, turning back to the area of the oscillator.

When he was out of immediate view, I let out the breath I had been holding. My shoulders and neck ached with tension. "I thought he was going to sack us," I breathed.

"Naw. He's a rational man. That was strange, though. What do you think Mr. Sharp was doing here?"

I shrugged. "Curious, I'm sure. Like everyone else in town."

Tesla called out from the other side of the room. "Cora, I have something for you to do."

My heart skipped a beat with excitement. I longed to help with one of his important experiments, not type out more notes. This was the moment I had been waiting for.

I turned away from Harrison, then snapped my head back for a quick question. "Where is Wolf this morning?"

"I think he and Mr. Tesla came to an arrangement. Because Wolf has other jobs to do around town, he's to come in the evenings twice a week. I'll see you later." Harrison brushed my arm with his fingertips as he turned toward a stack of empty crates I hadn't noticed to the side of the door.

"What are you doing today?" I asked.

"Hauling these away, then off to class. Good luck. Don't keep him waiting for long." He smiled, indicating the direction of Tesla's voice with a sweep of his head.

I smiled, feeling a little uneasy at being left alone with a man who was essentially a stranger to me. Without Wolf or Harrison, there would only be Mr. Tesla and me in this cavernous lab. With measured steps, I walked inside the circular portion of the room that contained the oscillator and coils. The instruments hummed with power. A thrill of excitement trailed across my belly. Mr. Tesla was seated in an uncomfortable-looking folding chair, his head bent over a notebook, long legs crossed at the ankles.

"What can I do for you, sir?" My voice sounded small in the space.

He continued to regard his notes as he answered my question with a question of his own. "Can you do calculations? And to what level?"

My excitement compounded. Goosebumps rose on my arms. I took a deep breath before answering. "Yes, sir. I'm currently learning calculus with Mr. Hill and am at the top of the class." This bordered on boasting, but it seemed important he should know my capabilities. It was the same as any man would do, so I kept my head high, refusing to feel shame for my accomplishments.

"Excellent. I have no time for things like budgets and need help balancing my bank book, which you'll find along with a pile of receipts on the table in the back room. I'm afraid I'm in a bit of a pickle."

I tried to keep my disappointment hidden, turning to do as he bid. Overcome, I turned back to Tesla. "Sir, my apologies. I was under the impression you required a laboratory assistant. If what you require is a secretary, perhaps I could help you find someone better suited." My heart pounded in my chest. I was doing the very opposite of what I had decided after speaking with Mr. Hill, but balancing receipts seemed a waste of my time.

Tesla raised his warm, brown eyes to mine. For a moment, I thought he would throw me out, a storm still passing behind his gaze. Until he smiled softly. "I understand, Miss Croft. You wish to do something more worthy of you, or something you imagine more worthy.

Patience is not a virtue of mine, either. At the moment, I'm working on recalculating a few things. When I'm satisfied, you may assist me in the experimentation. For now, the best thing you can do for me is balance my books. If I lose too much money, all of this will come to a halt. Mr. Williams was responsible for the receipts, and I haven't touched them since he left."

This was the most Mr. Tesla had said to me yet. I was satisfied with his explanation, but the reference to Mr. Williams left me a little shaken. How well did he know the man? Did he know anything about his death? I wanted to ask all this and more, only I was sure Mr. Tesla wouldn't react well to being questioned. "Of course, sir. I'll begin right away."

One more menial task, then I could help with the real science.

In my mind, I pictured a few receipts, neatly stacked. I was not prepared for the scattered, mountainous pile that awaited me in the anteroom. My household, which employed eight people, must have many more expenses. However, I had never in my life seen any evidence of it. Mother kept the books in a manner much like everything else: meticulous. I rubbed my eyes as I sat in the hard-backed chair. The sooner I began, the sooner I would finish.

By the time I balanced the final receipt, my father's pocket watch, which I carried today in my pocket, told me two hours had passed since the minute I sat at the table. I bustled around the small room after I finished, tidying up. I knew well enough after only one and a half days in the lab to wait for Mr. Tesla to come for me.

As I re-organized a cabinet, my back to the door, light footsteps tapped the ground behind me. I expected the newcomer to be Wolf, who walked with a light tread despite his giant status, but immediately caught the floral scent of an expensive French perfume. A perfume I had borrowed more than once. I whirled around.

"Dove, what on earth are you doing here? Did Mr. Tesla allow you admittance?" I whispered, waves of dread filling my belly.

Dove looked amused, her blue eyes sparkling. "I knocked on the open door, but no one came. Honestly, Cora, don't worry so. I only wanted to see what all the fuss was about."

"Did you know Mr. Sharp was here this morning?" I pulled her through the door.

Her eyes widened. "I didn't. What was he here for?" She moved into the room, her fine gown of mint-green silk peeking beneath her winter coat of white wool.

"The same as you, apparently. Everyone's curious about this place. But now that you've seen it, you must leave. Dove, Mr. Tesla hates intruders." I dared a look out the door, terrified to see Tesla's red face as he discovered yet another resident of town poking around his lab.

Dove giggled. "I'm hardly an intruder, Cora." Her gaze darted around the room.

I moved up to my friend and grasped her hands, bringing her focus onto me. "Of course, you're not, but my position here is tenuous at best. Anything could upset Mr. Tesla. It's been a trying morning. Please go, Dove."

She smirked, her eyes meeting mine. "Fine. I don't understand what the fuss is about, anyway. I'll pick you up a pastry from Mrs. King. I'm heading there to taste cakes. Kisses." Dove leaned forward, planting a peck on each of my cheeks.

"Let me make sure the coast is clear." I moved around her, tension knotting my brow. Dove giggled behind me. I wanted to be angry with her but knew she meant no harm. Dove lived for the moment, not taking consequences much into effect.

Tesla's back was to us as he stood in front of the oscillator, scribbling in his notebook. How he had missed Dove, I couldn't begin to imagine. He must have been completely absorbed in his work. The scent of her perfume was likely masked by the electrical smells of the lab.

I gestured for Dove to go. She touched me lightly on the arm as she passed, she winked, an amused look on her face. She tiptoed the length of the lab. The rustle of her skirts seemed louder to me than the banging of a drum. I didn't take a breath until she finally stepped out the door. Tesla took no notice.

The anteroom began to feel like my office. Even so, it closed in on me. Before I could sink into a chair, another commotion outside rose me back up. My fear was realized, Dove was found out.

My jaw clenched, muscles tense as I darted into the main lab. I collected myself when I realized the ruckus was caused by Harrison and two delivery men unloading new crates into the lab. The men went about their business quickly. Tesla walked over, standing close to where they were unloading their burden, scrutinizing a piece of paper Harrison handed to him. I joined him, remaining silent, hoping he would give me a new task.

When the men finished, Tesla signed one of the papers he held then handed it to the closest delivery man. One man, who stood sentinel near the door, looked around as much as his time allowed. After they had gone, Harrison took a crowbar, opening each crate for Tesla to inspect the contents.

I peered over Mr. Tesla's shoulder. The materials looked like nothing but a bunch of junk to me—wires, pieces of metal, and tools. To Mr. Tesla, these were the building blocks he needed to conduct his experiments.

Tesla nodded, chewing on the inside of his cheek as he went from crate to crate. "Everything appears to be in order, Mr. Byrne. You and Miss Croft will catalog and organize these materials onto the shelves at the far wall, then you may both leave for the day."

I inadvertently rolled my eyes at these seemingly petty tasks.

Tesla noticed. "Never fear, Miss Croft. I will have something else for you to do tomorrow. Tomorrow, we will be ready for another try. I will need solace this evening as I make sure everything is prepared."

He walked away. This, at last, sounded promising. I was sure he meant another try at an experiment that would fill the room with lightning. I took to my task of organizing with relish.

CHAPTER SEVEN

The day wore on. Unloading and organizing the crates took longer than I thought. We finished the last batch of materials as the light outside faded, my eyelids drooping with the sun. I prepared to leave the lab. The morning had been a pleasant one, weather wise, and I hadn't bothered to bring my coat. I was regretting that now as the temperatures were beginning to drop. All I wanted was to get home and rest. The drama-filled morning had led into an exhausting day, and I was ready to get into a hot bath.

"Blast." Tesla was wading through papers laid out over a table a few feet from where Harrison and I had finished our task. For such a brilliant man, he was terribly unorganized.

Harrison took a step toward our boss. "What is it, sir?"

Tesla raked his hands through his mass of dark hair, grabbing fistfuls and pulling. "A paper I was working on yesterday is gone. I know it was here this morning. Did either of you move anything on this table?"

Harrison shook his head as I spoke for both of us. "We know better than to touch any papers without permission. Besides, we've worked on organizing these bits all day." I indicated the metal shelves with a wave of my hand.

Tesla sighed, rubbing at his eyes so hard I was afraid he would hurt himself. "It was that Sharp," he said, more to himself than us.

I was afraid to say too much, to send him into a fit of anger. Still, I didn't think it was wise to jump to conclusions. "Mr. Sharp is a gentleman, Mr. Tesla. Perhaps it's best to take a step back and think through this with a rational mind."

Harrison looked at me with wide eyes, his head shaking back and forth. If he was cautioning me, it was too late, I had already spoken. How I longed to reach into the air and cram the words back in my mouth.

Tesla turned toward us, dark eyes rimmed with red.

Before he could speak, Harrison blurted out, "Besides, sir, there were people here today other than Mr. Sharp. The workers, and …" Harrison trailed off, looking back at me. Did he know Dove had briefly visited? My heart skipped a beat. Tesla was angry enough. I already had ties with one of the unwanted visitors, telling Tesla about a second didn't seem in my favor.

Tesla caught the morsel, urging Harrison to continue. "And?" he prompted.

Harrison turned away from me, my heart beating somewhere in my throat. He was going to rat me out. What other choice did he have? "Cora and me. And what about Marshall?" he finished.

The relief that washed over me was replaced by anger. My stomach was still twisted, but at least I could now breathe freely. Harrison was putting his position here on the line by keeping my secret about Dove. I wasn't sure why he would do this for me, but I was grateful. Instead of stopping there, he brought another friend into suspicion.

"That's nonsense. I've known Marshall all my life. He's the most honest, trustworthy person I know." I tried to measure my words, not allowing my emotion to show.

Harrison looked at me and shrugged. "I'm sorry, Cora. Honest people who need money turn to thievery all the time. Desperation is a tricky thing."

My anger was white-hot. I fisted my hands into the sides of my dress to keep from strangling this man who thought he was helping me. "Marshall is as innocent as I am."

"If you don't mind, I'll be the judge of who's innocent. Turn out your pockets, both of you." Tesla took a step toward us. "I'm sorry, but Harrison brings up a good point. After I'm satisfied you two are innocent, we can conduct a thorough search of the lab to be sure it wasn't laid elsewhere." Tesla stood in front of Harrison, arms crossed in front of his chest. Harrison emptied his pockets one by one. He turned out his pants pockets, then crossed to a chair where he had thrown his jacket. This he handed to Tesla. Tesla rummaged through its nooks and crannies.

"Shoes, please." Tesla handed the garment back to Harrison. The latter sat in the chair, pulled up his pants legs, and untied his shoes. When Tesla was satisfied, he turned toward me.

My dress contained only two pockets. Even so, I felt nervous, Tesla's hawk-like stare fixed on my person. I tried to tell myself he saw me with the same eyes he saw Harrison and there was nothing personal in his scrutinization. No doubt all his papers were of great importance. I shoved my hands into the recesses. I pulled out my watch and handed this to Tesla. Then, I yanked out the pockets themselves as far as I could. Tesla nodded, his gaze traveling around my figure. I squirmed under his cold glance.

"This is distasteful to me, Miss Croft, but I must be sure. Would you kindly remove your shoes, as well? I won't ask to look anywhere else."

I wanted to be indignant as much as I wanted to get this over with. I couldn't fault Tesla for wanting to find his important papers. Could I say I wouldn't be equally untrusting? Harrison rose from the chair so I could take his place, then politely turned his back.

I pulled my skirts up to mid-calf, kicking off my buckle shoes with the toe of each foot. Tesla bent over, peered inside the shoes, and nodded. At least that was now over.

"All right, Miss Croft. Thank you." He straightened his back, a red glow on his cheeks. "Will you please conduct a search of the anteroom while Mr. Byrne and I look in here? The paper in question has drawings of a new telescope design I've been working on."

I nodded, slipping my shoes back on and leaving the room with a quick step. The ordeal was as embarrassing for Tesla as it was for me. I still couldn't help but be a bit vexed, but I did as I was told and turned the anteroom upside down to find the elusive paper.

The drawing was familiar as I had transcribed it in my notes from the previous day. I thought back over the morning and our visitors. Dove had walked straight through the lab to where I was in the back room. She must have. Had she dallied, Tesla would have seen her. I was still amazed he hadn't. No wonder he was so easily stolen from.

Mr. Sharp could have no reason to take it, being a railroad man and not at all interested in electricity or scientific experimentation, that I knew of. The man was also among the wealthiest of my acquaintance. Selling the item for profit didn't make sense. The two delivery men had never ventured farther into the room than the space by the front door. Although one of the men seemed curious about what went on here, I didn't see how he had the opportunity. It was possible, however far-fetched, he stepped back inside while the rest of us were occupied.

Mr. Tesla rarely slept. The man was beset with troubling eccentricities and ailments, such as his strange flashes of light. The simplest explanation was that he had misplaced his document. A misunderstanding, pure and simple. When I was satisfied with my search, I joined the men in the main room.

Tesla was walking in circles around his oscillator, hands jammed into his pockets so far, I thought they would surely break free through the other end. He was mumbling to himself about something I couldn't make out.

Harrison moved next to me, worry creasing his brow. "Nothing. You?"

I shook my head, my eyes never leaving Tesla. Harrison groaned, massaging his neck and rolling it around in a circle. Tesla stopped and looked toward me. I gave him the same, sad shake of my head. He shut his eyes, renewing his pacing. Harrison and I stood silently waiting.

After a few tense moments, Tesla looked up and said, "That's all, I'm afraid."

"What do you mean?" I asked, new tension forming a knot between my shoulders. Did he mean we could leave for the day or leave permanently?

Tesla spoke with a far-off look in his eye. "I have done all I can here. Too much has happened."

"All that's happened is you've lost a piece of paper. Surely, you of all people remember what was on it." This was a bold tact to take with the man, but I didn't want this to end so soon.

Tesla sighed, looking into my eyes. "It's not one piece of paper, Miss Croft. It's three documents and one dead assistant."

It was foolish not to consider the loss of his laboratory assistant. "I'm sorry, Mr. Tesla. It was ruled an accident, was it not? The man's death, though sad and tragic, was no fault of yours." I thought of Joe Williams's body, crumpled and broken on the walk in front of his boarding house. The moment was so shocking, so brutal, I hadn't thought to look around much. From what I could remember, there didn't seem to be anyone else about except the landlady.

"I'm not sure it was an accident," he answered. Tesla continued to stand, his arms ramrod straight, hands thrust dangerously into the pockets of his pants. "The gentleman's demise was preceded by the loss of the second document a few days before. I accused him of taking it and another paper that was lost a month before that. It seemed logical given what I had to work with at the time. I dismissed him."

Tesla had a point, but did he have proof? "It is strange

how the events coincided in such a way. Did you ever find the first two papers?"

He shook his head. "No, and from what the police said, there were no papers found in his room, nor was I allowed to search it."

"Will you allow me to look into this, sir?" I surprised not only myself, but both men, as well.

"What?" Harrison spit out next to me.

I measured my words carefully before continuing. "I know everyone in this town. For example, the wife of the head of police regularly bakes wedding cakes. My friend Dove is going to see her today. I can make inquiries in a way that will seem like nothing more than childish curiosity, social gossip at worst. Perhaps I can get to the bottom of what's happening so you can stay and finish your work. Will you allow me one week to do this?" My motivation in doing so was selfish. If Tesla left so soon after I began working in his lab, I would never get to work on his experiments, nor would I be able to ask him to write me a letter. I needed him to remain in Colorado.

Both men stared at me, Tesla with more tact than Harrison, whose mouth was hanging open. Tesla shifted his gaze toward the ground. He rubbed his chin with one hand, the other on his hip. I remained silent while awaiting his decision. Harrison looked from me to Tesla, then back again, his lips still agape.

Tesla nodded at the floor before meeting my eyes. "All right, Miss Croft. I suppose one more week won't make any difference. Investigate all you like."

I didn't think I was expecting him to say yes. Part of me wanted to take it back. I wasn't equipped to investigate possible theft and a mysterious death. Or was I? A thought began to form in my mind as the three of us stared at each other. What was an investigation other than asking questions and talking with people? As a young woman who moved among the best society in Colorado Springs, I was uniquely qualified to inquire everyone I needed to.

"Very well, gentlemen. If you don't mind, I'll begin my questions with the two of you." Although my stomach was beginning to feel hollow from lack of food, I wanted to take advantage of having them both at my disposal.

Harrison shook his head, eyes rolling. Mr. Tesla smiled wide. "Good, Miss Croft. Let's not waste any time."

We moved to the anteroom, Tesla and Harrison seated across from me. A pad of paper and a pencil sat at the ready. Why not dive straight into this new role of detective? I asked Tesla to give me an account of each incident—where had the items gone missing, who had been around.

The first document, he explained, went missing from his room at the Alta Vista Hotel. The only person who had been in his room was the hotel's maid. Tesla had gotten to know the woman, Mary Wren, quite well. He required a lot in the way of special handling, it seemed. The woman delivered eighteen clean towels a day to Mr. Tesla's room. I remembered what Harrison had said about Tesla being obsessed with the number three: eighteen was divisible by three. He was sure the young woman must be innocent, as she couldn't read; the papers would mean nothing to her.

Tesla noticed nothing strange about the day, nor was anything else missing but the one document. The second paper disappeared from the lab. The only people who had been in and out of the lab the day the paper went missing were Tesla himself and his assistant, Joe Williams. None of this meant much, as Tesla did not seem to notice when visitors slipped through the often-open door. Anyone in town could be guilty.

"What do you know of Mr. Williams's death, Mr. Tesla?" I asked. There was no way to be gentle with this question. It had to be asked.

Tesla frowned, a shadow passing over his face. "It was so tragic. He was a young man with a promising future." He paused, looking at his hands. "The death was ruled accidental, but I don't see how it could have been."

"What do you mean?" I again saw Joe Williams sprawled

on the hard ground.

"I mean, Miss Croft, how does one trip on a rug five feet from a window, crash through the glass, and fall to the flagstone below?"

I swallowed the lump forming in my throat. "Is that what the police said happened?"

Mr. Tesla nodded, holding my gaze, hands folded one on top of the other. "It is. Doesn't seem very likely, does it?"

I shook my head. The version Tesla told me did not seem very likely at all. It seemed to me that if one trips on a rug that far from a window, they'd simply fall to the floor. "He couldn't have done it himself. Even if …" I trailed off, unsure of how to say what I was thinking. "Well, even if he had meant to harm himself, how could one throw themselves through a glass window?"

"Precisely, Miss Croft. The force needed to push through and break the glass would take an extreme amount of effort. Better to open the window if self-harm was the intention."

I sat back in my chair, momentarily stunned. I thought of the cuts on Joe Williams' face and head. "Are you saying, Mr. Tesla, you believe Joe Williams was murdered?" Of course, this was what he was saying. When faced with these questions, how could there be another explanation?

No matter what, I couldn't quite wrap my mind around this. A murder in Colorado Springs? And why was it being covered up? Joe Williams wasn't a wealthy man. He lived a modest life in a neat but small boarding home.

"I do. Murder is the only logical conclusion."

All this time, Harrison was sitting as still as a statue, his arms crossed across his chest. Now, he leaned forward. "I'm sorry, but this doesn't make sense. Why would the police cover up the murder of a good, respectable man? And why, Mr. Tesla, haven't you said anything?"

Tesla shrugged. "I can only answer your second question, Mr. Byrne. I went to the station only yesterday to demand to know what they were doing to bring Mr. Williams's killer to justice. The captain looked at me with a blank face and said, 'Who would we put on trial, the rug?' I was furious, incensed. I would have left town immediately had it not been for my research. Perhaps I gave up too easily. I'm too distracted with my own work." He looked at his hands again as he worked them together.

I reached out to pat his hand. "What could you have done, sir? If the case was closed, the case was closed."

After Tesla had said everything he could think of regarding Joe Williams, which was not of much help, I thought of Harrison. Harrison had only begun to work at the lab two weeks ago and knew nothing of Mr. Williams or the missing papers. I was afraid to ask him about the morning or anything he may have witnessed, so I left the subject for now.

The three of us adjourned our meeting. Tesla went back to his work. There was no rest for him. With Tesla out of the room, I turned to Harrison, who held his coat open for me.

"You can't ride home without an extra layer. The temperature is steadily dropping. Also, aren't you going to ask me about who I saw today, Miss Croft?" Another irksome smile. I turned my back to slip my arms into the wool sleeves, already too cold to argue. Harrison's coat smelled like fresh air and a hint of bergamot. I wondered if he was a tea drinker as I involuntarily moved my head to inhale the lapel. I righted myself quickly, hoping Harrison hadn't noticed.

"I already know what you saw or smelled. Yes, Dove Mackenzie was here. She only popped in because she was curious and wanted to see me. She was here for mere minutes before she left. Besides, what possible use could Dove have for a sketch of a telescope?" I turned back toward him, his large coat enveloping me like I was a small child.

"I'm not accusing your friend, Cora. Just pointing out

your omission." Harrison's hand lingered a little too long on my shoulder. I shrugged it off as I turned to leave. "Not so fast. I intend to help you with your crazy scheme."

My head snapped sharply in his direction. The coat, several sizes too large, slid off one shoulder. "What do you mean? How could you possibly help me?"

Harrison, popping his hat on his head, paused long enough to fix me in his gaze. "I can help with the police, for one thing. My dad's a cop. And it's good to have a partner. You don't know what you may be getting yourself into."

I had forgotten Harrison's father was a police officer. This could prove very helpful, maybe even more so than a conversation with Mrs. King. I narrowed my eyes, snatched my riding gloves from a chair, and passed them from one hand to the other. "Very well. Be at my house first thing tomorrow. Tell Mother you're there to take me to the library at the college."

CHAPTER EIGHT

Colorado College was an easy excuse. It was the school Mother preferred I attend. She was thrilled I would be spending the afternoon on campus grounds.

"You're dressing awfully plainly these days, Cora. Why not wear your new rose silk?" She was shuffling through the gowns in my wardrobe as I tied a simple gray bonnet over my brown tresses. Mother, practical as she was, also wanted society to understand we were still among the wealthiest in town. Practicality did have its limits.

"I'm studying, Mother, not courting," I said as I surveyed my figure clad all in gray.

"You look like a storm cloud, and who said anything about courting? I'll tell Walters to get the buggy ready, or do you prefer to ride Lady?" She moved to the door.

"Don't bother. Mr. Byrne is coming to pick me up."

Mother stopped abruptly, turning toward me. "Is he?"

"Yes, dear. We're partnering on a project for school." I smiled primly, kissing my mother on the cheek before I strode for the door.

I walked with my head held high down the stairs. Truth be told, I felt anything but confident. My belief that I would be able to get answers where others had failed began to crumble. How could a seventeen-year-old girl succeed where professionals had not? Still, I had to try. I didn't want Mr. Tesla to leave town. Not when I'd only begun to work for him. A sort of protectiveness for him surged through me. All his efforts here would be for naught. As capable a man as he was, he needed someone to help keep a watchful eye over the chaos of his life. He was too focused on his work to shield himself from the nefarious designs of others. I would do what I could to help him as long as he remained in Colorado.

The morning was bright, the weather mild. Not a flake of snow remained anywhere. The clear snap of the fresh air greeted me as soon as I was outside. This was often how it was in Colorado Springs, the weather changing minute by minute. With Halloween only three weeks away, I wondered if we would have a white Halloween or a sunny one. Either was equally possible.

Harrison Byrne sat on the seat of his buggy, tall and unbending. His gaze was trained straight ahead as if he were watching something of interest. This gave me a moment to regard him as I made my way down the flagstone walk. I had to admit he was a good-looking man, in a rough sort of way. His profile was pleasing enough. That mop of dark hair, neatly swept back from his face, was casually charming, and there was that one errant lock, which always fell forward, covering his eyebrows. He often tried to push the lock back into place without success.

As I neared, he snapped his head toward me. A wide grin melted across his face. Harrison jumped from his seat in one swift movement, all arms and legs. "Would you like to sit in the back, Lady Croft, or up front with the likes of this peasant?" He was joking, but I didn't find his brand of humor amusing. No one else had ever caused me to blush one moment and groan with irritation the next.

"Don't call me Lady Croft. I'll sit with you, peasant or not." I ignored the hand he offered, grabbing hold of the side of the buggy instead, and hauled myself up. With my feet planted inside, I tried to stand, but my skirt was caught somewhere behind me. I reached back to pull on the fabric, nothing budged.

"Allow me, please, Lady Croft—I mean, Cora." Harrison snickered as he lifted the hem of my skirt over the door latch.

I mumbled my thanks, moving to sit on the passenger side. When we were both seated, rumbling down the road, I said, "How receptive to answering our questions do you think your father will be?"

Harrison shrugged. "My dad's a man of many moods. It all depends on how we find him on this day."

This didn't sound promising. Officer Byrne was unknown to me, so there was no way for me to prepare.

We trotted along the streets, the green of summer giving way to the brown of winter. We cruised right past the college library Isabella thought was our destination. A nervousness to once again come across Maxwell Priest fluttered through me. I shrank back against the seat, my gaze scanning the area. The brick building was bustling with serious-looking students in the early morning. I didn't spy Mr. Priest, which I counted as lucky.

The center of town was as it always was—busy. People walked along the road lined with horses and buggies, the many buildings serving as workplaces for some. The streets were pungent with horse droppings, obliterating the fresh mountain air. Automobiles were a rather new invention, and I wondered if we would see more in the coming year or if they would be nothing more than a fad, as Isabella thought. There were two of these contraptions in town. One belonged to Timothy Sharp and one to Dove's father. Mr. Mackenzie rarely took it out, feeling it was too unpredictable for him to handle.

The county jail housed our city's police officers and the odd inmate or two. Harrison pulled over, across the street from the building, and once again leaped from his seat. I was momentarily jealous of the freedom of movement his clothing afforded him. As Harrison tied Rex to the hitching post, I helped myself down from the buggy. It was best to avoid Harrison's clasp around my waist.

Inside the building, my shoes clicked loudly on the marble floor, each footstep echoing through the foyer of the small room. A great plaster mural of Colorado's coat of arms loomed ahead. The shiny pate of a man in uniform happened to sit in the dead center of the crossed pickaxes represented at the bottom of this coat of arms. I stifled a laugh. As the bald man looked up from the desk in the center of the room, toast crumbs fell onto his shirt.

"Hello, Harrison," he called out. "Come to see your dad?"

Harrison moved up to the desk, a step ahead of me. "Yes, Mr. Greenville. Is he here?"

Mr. Greenville went back to eating his toast, inclining his head to the right. "At his desk," he mumbled, his mouth crammed full.

I tried not to make a face as I followed Harrison. Never had I been inside the county jail. Not only did I have no idea where we were going, but I was also a little nervous to face a room full of police officers, irrational though it may be. I chewed my bottom lip.

Colorado Springs wasn't a big city like some other places, and we didn't have a large police force. The huge space, empty of décor except for the flags of our nation and state that stood along the entryway, seemed rather cold, which had nothing to do with the temperature. Inside the cavernous room, a handful of men in uniform sat at desks. Two read the newspaper and two played cards, their chairs pushed together.

I spotted Harrison's dad right away. Harrison and this man could have been twins, only one was twenty years younger. The elder Mr. Byrne slid his eyes toward his son, folding his newspaper neatly. He laid it in front of him. Mr. Byrne remained seated, his hands clasped over the folded paper. "What are you doing here? Don't you have to work this morning?"

Harrison stopped in his tracks. This was the first time I'd seen him so unsure. I stepped forward and noticed his eyes dip to the floor. "I've hired Mr. Byrne's buggy for the day. Cora Croft." I stuck out my hand.

Officer Byrne stood, grasping my hand in his. "Pleased to meet you, Miss Croft. Can I ask what brings you to the jail?" Harrison's dad indicated the wooden swivel chair next to his desk.

The chair squawked as I sat, spinning it toward Officer Byrne. "Joe Williams was a school friend and acquaintance. I was wondering if you could tell me more about how he died." I wasn't sure how one asked questions of a police officer, but by the look on Officer Byrne's face—half confusion, half surprise, with eyebrows drawn together and eyes wide—I guessed that wasn't it.

Harrison sat propped with one hip on the end of his father's desk behind my shoulder. "Miss Croft isn't known for her tact, Dad," he joked, bringing a flush to my cheeks. "She's concerned some details were overlooked is all." Harrison seemed to have recovered from his uncertainty.

I had to wonder what his relationship with his dad was like. Officer Byrne blinked a couple of times, looking from his son back to me. He sat with a frown. "Overlooked? Maybe you could be more specific, Miss Croft."

I cleared my throat, leaning slightly toward the officer. "It was said Joe tripped on a rug several feet from his closed window, fell through the glass, and onto the walk. You must admit, this doesn't seem a very likely scenario, Officer Byrne."

Officer Byrne surveyed the room in front of him, then shifted in his seat, moving in toward me. In a low voice, he said, "I wouldn't know, as it wasn't my case. This isn't the sort of thing a lady should be concerning herself with. And you—" He moved his attention to his son. "I'll thank you not to surprise me at work again. Good morning to you both."

I opened my mouth to protest as Harrison put his hand on my shoulder. "Come on, Cora," he said softly.

Disappointed, I stood stiffly. We left the room without so much as a look around. My first foray into an investigation was a complete disaster. In the foyer, Harrison tugged at my elbow. I turned to face him. "That was a waste of time. How can we expect to learn anything about what really happened if this is the kind of treatment we can expect?" I sighed in frustration. "And please, never patronize me like that again."

"I didn't mean to patronize you. I could tell by the look on Dad's face that he was a little shocked by your question. We'll have to dig deeper. I apologize for my dad. I was wrong in assuming he would help us." Harrison shoved his hands in his pockets, rocking back and forth on his heels. He whispered, "I have an idea, but I'm not sure you're going to like it."

Before I could ask him to clarify, an officer approached us with a quick step. He was the second man who had been reading the day's paper not far from where Mr. Byrne sat. The man, several inches shorter than me, appeared to be walking right for us. Before careening into me, he took off at another angle, but not before pressing something into my hand. He zoomed by so fast, a draft caught my skirt, sending it fluttering behind me.

"Hey, watch where you're going," Harrison called to his back. "That was strange. You all right, Cora?"

My hand tightened around the folded paper. "Fine. Let's go, shall we? Tell me your idea at the buggy."

I scurried out of the jail, Harrison a step behind me. I streaked across the street, not taking particular care of who was coming and going. My mind was so preoccupied with what the note could contain that I didn't see the horse and buggy heading right for me. The driver had to rein in his horse to avoid trampling me. A loud curse fell from his lips. I continued without a word.

"Whoa, Cora," Harrison called after me, dodging people

and horses to keep up. "Watch where you're going."

Breathless, I reached Rex. Holding onto his reins, I rested my forehead on his cheek.

"What's gotten into you?" Harrison breathed into my ear.

My gaze met his. "I'm not sure, but I think something terribly exciting just happened."

Harrison crinkled his brow, his mouth turned downward. "Almost being trampled by a horse and buggy is exciting?"

I shook my head and held up my hand. Grasped in my fingers was the piece of paper passed to me in the foyer of the jail.

Harrison shrugged. "What is it?"

"I've no idea. The officer who nearly knocked me over pressed it into my hand."

Harrison's eyes lit up. He stepped back, offering me his hand. "Get in."

Within moments, we were pulling away from the jailhouse. A couple of blocks over, Harrison once again pulled Rex to a stop. "Okay. Let's see it."

With eager fingers, I unfolded the note, holding it out so we could both read. "Not easy to make out, is it?"

Harrison squinted at the paper. "No, he was clearly in a hurry when he wrote this."

I scrutinized the scrawl a moment longer. The words were barely more than chicken scratch. The daily goings-on of downtown were busy all around us. The noise barely registered as I focused on the note. "I'm fairly certain it's an address—800 Bijou St. Followed by the number three. Is he telling us to be at this address at three o'clock?"

"It seems that way." Harrison slumped back. His hand went to his mouth, and he began chewing on his nails. "I don't like this, Cora. It's too underhanded," he said between bites.

I batted his hand from his mouth. "Stop that. Maybe it is a little odd, but there's something this man wants to tell us. We must know what it is, Harrison. What if it's the information we need? We could find out who was behind the death of Joe Williams and the theft of Tesla's documents with one conversation. We owe it to both men to discover the truth."

Harrison shook his head. "What if the man who gave you this is the killer? We're walking right into a trap."

I laughed. "Don't be so dramatic. The man's an officer of the law. Not everything is sinister. We'll bring Wolf with us. He's strong and he knows what's going on."

Harrison sighed, looking away. "Fine. Safety in numbers is a good idea, at least."

"What were you going to tell me before this happened? Your idea?"

"Yeah. At the time, it seemed dangerous in a fun way. Now it seems dangerous in a stupid way."

"What?" I prodded.

"I was going to suggest we break into Joe's apartment. Look around. Maybe we can find something the cops missed."

I grinned, bumping Harrison's shoulder with my own. "A brilliant idea. I'm ashamed I didn't think of it. Does this mean you're all in, Mr. Byrne?"

Harrison met my eyes, smirking. "Let's take one thing at a time. Where can we find Marshall?"

CHAPTER NINE

A search for Wolf was no easy task. The man could easily have been at any number of locations. We stopped first at his home on the south side of town, where he lived with his mom and two siblings in a modest blue A-frame cottage.

His sister, Michelle, was beating a rug draped over a wire in the front yard, a dirt-streaked apron tied around the front of her brown dress. She stopped and waved as Harrison and I pulled up to the house.

I stepped down to meet her, grasping her hands and kissing her on the cheek. "Good morning, Michelle. I'm looking for Wolf and hope it won't take hours to find him."

She laughed. "Lucky for you, I know just where he is. He's at Anne Marie's house this morning. I believe they're closer to finally setting a date."

This was wonderful news. Anne Marie lived right around the corner. I sighed in relief. "I'm so happy to hear that. I know she's been patient for some time."

Michelle giggled.

"Do you mind if we leave the buggy here for a few minutes?"

"Of course not, Cora. I may even have a sugar cube or two for this guy." Michelle walked over to Rex to scratch his ears, who was grateful for the attention, leaning his big head into her hand.

Harrison and I walked the short distance on the dirt road to where Anne Marie lived in a similar house with her grandparents. The last time I saw her, she joked they would be happy to see her married and moving out. Anne Marie was older than Wolf by a few years, and her grandmother long chided her for being an old maid. Although Anne Marie made light of the teasing, I suspected she was ready to move on.

The pair were seated side by side on the porch, with Wolf holding Anne Marie's hand in his. He watched us warily as we walked up the front path.

"Good morning, you two. Michelle said the big day is nearing?" I winked at Anne Marie, who smiled warmly.

Her lovely tanned skin glowed with a happiness that surely came from within. "A Christmas wedding, Cora. I can't wait to finally be this man's wife." She beamed Wolf a smile, who shyly grinned at the ground.

"That's the best news. Congratulations to you both." I paused, wanting to take a moment between this beautiful announcement and the strange request I was about to make. "I came over to ask you for some help, Wolf. Feel free to decline, as I realize it's all a bit bizarre."

Harrison and I stood on the steps of the small porch as I related what happened the day before at Tesla's lab and that very morning at the county jail.

"You want me to go with you two as you break into a dead man's boarding room and speak to a police officer?" Wolf looked me straight in the eyes, his brows raised in approbation.

"When you say it like that, it makes me rethink our plan. But, yes, Harrison thinks it will be helpful to have safety in numbers, especially when we meet the mysterious officer." I didn't think this sounded too unreasonable.

"Cora, I'll gladly go with you to meet the officer. I agree with Harrison at least that far. As for the boarding house—

no, I can't help you there."

I pursed my lips, crossing my arms across my chest. "I don't see …" I began.

Harrison put his hand on my arm. "Marshall will stand out in that neighborhood, Cora. And, if we get caught, he'll catch it a lot worse than we will. I'm the son of a police officer, and you're a belle of the Springs. Besides, I doubt his fiancée would appreciate us getting him into trouble so soon before their wedding."

I looked down at the ground.

Harrison continued. "Cora and I will go to the apartment. Marshall can meet up with us afterward. How does that sound to everyone?"

Wolf agreed, looking to Anne Marie for the final word. She nodded, dropping a kiss on his cheek. "Just be careful," she said softly.

"All right. Thank you for helping us, Wolf. I didn't think of what we would be asking of you. And, Anne Marie, we won't get him into any trouble, promise. I'll look out for him as I would my own brother."

Wolf smiled. "And that's why I've always liked you so much, Cora. I'm happy to help you and Mr. Tesla. Like you, he only sees a person when he looks at me, not someone from the wrong side of town."

Harrison shuffled next to me. "What about me?" he said under his breath.

Wolf jumped up to clap Harrison on the back. I laughed. It felt good after the stress of the last couple of days.

The boarding house was a lovely three-story home on Cascade Avenue. The yellow house with white shutters and a white painted porch was quiet and serene as we walked up the front path. All evidence of the gruesome scene was now long gone. A songbird sat perched in the oak tree gracing the front yard, singing to us as we approached.

Rex was waiting for us a block away. We wanted to

remain as inconspicuous as possible. Joe lived on the third floor in the attic room. Our cover, should we be stopped, was that of potential boarders. The closer we drew to the front door, the shallower my breathing became. I began to wonder what on earth we were thinking. We wouldn't get two feet inside the building before the mistress descended upon us.

Harrison and I tiptoed up the front steps. I was worried our feet would cause the boards of the porch to creak, but they remained silent. Upon reaching the door, Harrison turned to look at me, his gaze intent on mine. I nodded with surety I didn't feel.

He grasped the doorknob gingerly, twisting it by small degrees until the door clicked open. My pulse picked up speed as he pushed it inward. I shoved my head in first, looking one way then the other. Empty.

I crept inside the entryway, Harrison right behind me. He pulled the door, leaving it partially open behind us to ease our escape.

The little foyer was homey, inviting. A walnut hall tree sat off to the side, holding a small collection of hats, canes, and scarves. If I was going by hats alone, there appeared to be three people at home. The stairs ahead were carpeted. This would help muffle the tread of our boots as we ascended. We couldn't afford to wait any longer where we could easily be discovered, so we made for the steps.

The staircase wound from the front of the house to the back then around to the front again. By the time we reached the closed attic room, I realized I had been holding my breath, and I slowly exhaled. There didn't seem to be a soul about.

I reached for the doorknob this time, my heart pounding with the excitement. Of course, it was locked. I was ready to pull a pin from my hair when Harrison pulled a small bundle from his pocket. He knelt to lay the roll of fabric on the dark wood floor. Harrison extracted an odd-looking pick along with a tool, which looked like tweezers, then pushed them into the lock.

"Where did you get those?" I whispered.

"My father sometimes brings things home from work. This set was confiscated from a man who tried to rob the bank." He worked the tools inside the lock, his brow furrowed in concentration.

I was impressed. These tools were far superior to my simple hairpin. After a couple of seconds of jiggling the lock, a satisfying click sounded. I peered nervously down the winding staircase; my ears open to the sound of anyone below.

"Got it." Harrison slipped the tools back in his pocket.

We couldn't get inside the room fast enough. The space was not as I expected. Instead of minimal and plain, as I would have imagined a bachelor's room to be, it was as warm and lovely as the foyer downstairs.

A single four-poster bed covered with a blue bedspread stood to the right of the window. A bureau in warm cherry sat next to the door, topped with a ceramic ewer and washbasin. There were doilies on the arms of the overstuffed armchair; painted mountain scenes graced the walls. The room appeared all in order except for the braided rug and the window.

"It doesn't look like anything, but the window has been touched. Have the police even searched the room?" Harrison was taking in the space as I was.

I shook my head, unsure of how to answer. He was right. If the room had been searched by the police, they cleaned up well after themselves. The only evidence anyone had been here was the boards nailed over the broken windowpane.

"Try to disturb as little as possible," I whispered. "And try to walk quietly. We don't know who or what is beneath this room."

There wasn't much to search. I broke off, pulled in the direction of the bureau. The piece had three drawers, each of which I carefully rummaged through. There was nothing but men's clothing. I peered into the ewer—nothing.

Harrison was feeling around the armchair, pulling out the cushion to look under.

"The rug hasn't even been straightened," I observed. "Don't you find that odd?"

Harrison grunted a reply. "Look how far it is from the window. Ludicrous to think Joe tripped from the middle of the room and was somehow launched ten feet through a glass pane."

My heart rate was beginning to pick up again. The thought was ludicrous, indeed. It wasn't quite ten feet, closer to five, but he was correct. "The window is a rather small one. I suppose it would make sense if he tripped, then went headfirst through the window. But to have the momentum to keep going, for his entire body to clear the windowsill, he would have to be moving at a breakneck speed."

"It would also make sense for him to grab at something as he fell, yet the curtains are undisturbed." Harrison walked over to the pretty lace curtains, moving them back with his hand. "There's nothing here, Cora. Whether the police have been here or not …" He trailed off his sentence, bringing the curtain up to his nose.

"What?" I prodded.

He shook his head. "Nothing. I thought I smelled something floral for a moment, like a perfume."

I stood by the bed. "Funny. All I smell are cigarettes." With my nose wrinkled to protect myself from the awful smell, I bent down to take a peek underneath the perfectly made bed. Once again, nothing was to be found. Wanting a closer look, I set my hands on the floor and moved down to my knees. As I did so, I felt something under my palm. I moved my hand back, discovering the source of the smell in the process. "Ash." I peered under the bed, spying the rest of the contaminant. The stubbed-out cigarette was sitting behind one of the bed's posts.

Harrison handed me a handkerchief from his breast

pocket. I stood, wiping my hands. "For as neat as this place is, I'm surprised Joe would leave ash and a cigarette on the floor. Whatever happened, it seems clearer now. This death was no accident. The rug is too far from the window, which was closed, and too small for a man to have fallen out of on his own." I looked at Harrison, who was staring intently at the rug.

"How could no one have heard anything?" he muttered. "Someone wants to throw me out a window, you better believe I'm making all kinds of racket."

I shrugged. "It would depend on what time of day and who was here, I suppose. The hour was late morning. Perhaps the rest of the household was out. The mistress was here, though. I saw her run down the front steps, but that doesn't mean she was inside. The house is awfully quiet right now."

Harrison nodded. I was about to suggest we leave when the door opened, sending my stomach into my throat. The bird-like mistress of the house, all hard angles and ruffles, stood in front of us.

"What on earth?" she began.

I didn't let her get far. "Good afternoon, ma'am. My brother was interested in renting this room." Would she recognize me? I moved forward with my hand stuck out in front of me. "Sadly, the room is too small for his needs."

The lady looked at my hand without shaking it. "How did you know a room was available? And how did you get up here? Sneaking about, no doubt."

"Not at all, ma'am. There was no one around, and the door was open. I'm so sorry if we've made a mistake. We'll leave you alone now."

"Wait a minute. Have you been smoking in here? I don't allow smoking indoors."

I looked sharply at Harrison. "No, ma'am. We assumed the cigarette smell was left over from the previous tenant."

"Mr. Williams smoked the occasional cigar, but always did so on the back porch. My tenants obey the rules of this house. I despise cigarettes. If my renters are caught smoking, they're told to move out, no exceptions. Now, I think it's time you both leave."

I looked at Harrison, inclining my head. With a mad thought racing through my mind, I dropped his handkerchief on the ground. As I stooped to pick it up, I scooped up the cigarette. What made me do this, I couldn't say. Harrison was hot on my heels as I edged around the woman.

"No one's been in here since it happened," she muttered to herself, moving farther into the room.

I stopped abruptly. Harrison ran into my back. We stood in an awkward position, but the moment was too perfect to pass up. I turned, pushing Harrison back a step. With sweet innocence, I asked, "Since what happened?"

The woman shook her head, looking around the room. "He was such a kind man, never any trouble. Paid his dues every other Friday, like clockwork. To have such a tragedy occur on my premises is beyond me."

I swallowed, wondering how I could prod her to continue.

Harrison took over. "Yes, I believe I heard about what happened here. A man fell to his death, an accident, I believe. These things happen."

The woman snickered. "Wasn't no accident, at all. The story those policemen made up was just that … a story. At first, they thought Mr. Williams was murdered. I heard them talking about it through the vent."

I pictured this lady with her ear pressed against the vents, listening to the daily conversations of her renters. She likely knew every little secret of everyone living in these walls.

"Why would they change their mind, I wonder." My voice was quiet. I wanted to encourage her to keep talking.

She shrugged. "Don't know. It wasn't until the third one came that the tune was changed."

"Third one?"

"A man in a suit, said he was a copper from Denver. He

said it was an accident, pure and simple. Scared me a little, he did. I agreed what happened was as he said. Don't want any trouble." This whole time, she was looking off into the distance as if in a reverie. After she spoke the last line, she snapped her head toward us, as if coming back into herself.

"And you two were smoking in my room? Clear out before I get the police back here." She shooed us out.

Harrison and I moved as one out the door, down the stairs, and out the front of the charming boarding house with the not-so-charming mistress. We continued to walk side by side down the walk, our feet moving fast.

"What do you make of all that?" he asked once we were heading down the street toward Rex.

I had several thoughts over the course of the last few minutes, and the cigarette was still inside the handkerchief clutched in my hand. "The third person to come to the room, do you think he was a police officer?"

"No, Cora, I don't."

A shiver went through me. "That man must be our killer."

Harrison came to a halt, pulling me to a stop by my elbow. "We're out, Cora. Something is going on here, something deadly dangerous. Can you hear yourself? We're talking about killers, and cops who did his bidding. This is madness."

"You may be out, and that's up to you. But I'm seeing this through to the end. Helping Tesla is secondary now. A man was murdered and no one else seems interested in bringing his killer to justice." I stubbornly stood in front of Harrison, my face hard.

He sighed, rubbing his eyes with his knuckles. "You'll be the death of us," he murmured, turning away from me.

"Don't say that—it's bad luck. Say a prayer, quick."

At that, Harrison laughed out loud. "You're an interesting mix of practical and superstitious, Cora Croft." He held his hand out to me. "Get in and let's pick up Marshall. At the very least, we can get today over with and then figure out what to do."

CHAPTER TEN

Wolf was waiting for us precisely where he said he'd be. The park across from the school was a little center of calm in the middle of our bustling town. Ladies leisurely walked bundled up in mufflers and mitts while gentlemen hurried from one place to another.

Wolf sat on a bench near the road, watching the ground in front of him. He had my Willow. Holding the reins, Harrison jumped from the buggy and jogged over to where Wolf sat. I watched from several feet away as the two men exchanged words. I couldn't make out what they said but could tell from the scrunched-up look on Wolf's face that he was no happier about our little adventure. After a couple of minutes of what must have been grumbling, he stood and made his way toward the buggy alongside Harrison.

"All right, Cora," Wolf said as he put Willow on the floor of the buggy. "Let's get this over with. I stopped by your house to help Walters shoe the horses and your mother wanted Willow to get some exercise. She didn't know I was coming to see you."

After handing the reins back to Harrison, I turned around on my seat with a smile for Wolf and a kiss for my dog. "Wonderful. Willow will have to wait in the buggy while we talk with the officer, then we can take her elsewhere to walk. Thank you, Wolf. This will be easy and quick, you'll see."

Wolf tucked his hands underneath his thighs with a grunt, looking to the side, back toward the park. We continued on our way. Acacia Park sat between Tejon and Nevada Avenues, which ran north and south, and Platte and Bijou Streets, which ran east and west.

We turned east on Bijou. The address we had been given wasn't far, only a few blocks. I leaned back, scratching my dog's warm ears as she fell asleep at Wolf's feet. Within minutes, we pulled up to a small house, which better resembled a cube. Butterflies crowded in my stomach for the second time that day.

"Are you ready for this?" Harrison looked at me, then Wolf.

All I could do was nod, my eyes attached to the front of the little house. The home, which appeared as a brown speck between two much larger, more colorful homes, was the only house on the block with a cold chimney. All the others had healthy billows of smoke venting into the cold air. The man must live alone. I couldn't imagine a family gathered inside around a cold hearth.

The brick walkway was uneven and in dire need of being replaced. If one wasn't careful, a nasty spill could be taken. There was an uncared-for look to the yard and exterior of the house, which became more pronounced the closer we drew to the front door. Wolf lagged behind us. He was with us, but only grudgingly.

It seemed unspoken that I would be the one to take charge, since I had been given the note. I took a deep breath, squaring my shoulders, and knocked three times on the cracked, wooden door. Clasping my hands in front of me, I waited for the small man from the jail to answer. No one came. I shuffled my feet, glancing back at my companions, then raised my hand to knock again. Before my knuckles could rap the hard surface, someone pulled it open, catching me off guard.

Harrison reached out to grab hold of my waist as I tipped forward. My face flushed as I brushed his hands from my body. I was about to address Harrison when instead my eyes landed on the man from the jail. "Uh, hello," I stammered out the words as I looked the officer over.

This was the same individual, although he appeared quite changed in the span of only a few hours. His face, shiny with sweat, was white as a ghost. Small eyes appeared even smaller by the heavy droop of his lids. A line of spittle was clinging to his chin, threatening to break free at any moment. He clutched at his belly, drops of what appeared to be blood splattered his open shirt collar.

I heard Wolf behind me take two audible steps backward, muttering my name under his breath. Harrison reached up, touching my elbow with his fingertips. He spoke first. "Our apologies, sir, you're unwell. Come away, Cora. We'll visit another time."

I felt rooted to my spot, horrified yet unable to move.

"I was fine … fine—this morning, before I ate my lunch. Now … this." The man seemed in a daze, looking right at me but not seeing me.

I knew we should leave, but something told me we would not get a second chance to question him. Perhaps his illness was what compromised his faculties, and once he recovered, he would think better of talking with us. "Sir, did you have something to tell me about the death of Joseph Williams?" It was brazen, rude even, but I couldn't turn around.

His eyes focused on mine. "Joseph Williams," he whispered.

I nodded, hoping to prod him on.

"Cora, this isn't the time," Harrison said, too close to my ear.

The man lifted his hand from his stomach to wipe the sweat dripping into his eyes. "Shouldn't have happened," he mumbled. "I shouldn't have said anything. That gloved devil with the cigarette. That demon will get me next."

With that, the sick man found the strength to slam the door in my face. The waft of air and the shaking of the frame pushed me to take a step back.

I whirled around, my eyes wide. "What happened?"

"It's obvious to me," Wolf began. "That man is end stage. Tuberculosis. You saw the blood on his shirt. Probably what brought him to Colorado in the first place. Anyway, he's delusional with it. Looks like he doesn't have much time left. Poor man."

What Wolf said partly made sense. Our city, along with Manitou Springs, was a haven for the poor souls afflicted with the dreaded disease. It was believed our dry air and mineral waters were healing for the sick who came here in droves. It was unlikely the man would have deteriorated so quickly, but perhaps I hadn't noticed his illness at the jail. Everything had happened so fast.

Wolf was already halfway to the buggy, not bothering to wait for the rest of us. Harrison held out his left hand, crooking his right behind me as if I needed to know which direction to go. Reluctantly, I walked forward.

"But what about what he said?" I asked Wolf's back. "The gloved devil with the cigarette. What could that mean except he's spoken with our killer?"

Wolf stood to the side, offering me his hand up. "Delusional madness, Cora," he said as I placed my hand in his. "What do you think is going on here? Some grand conspiracy?"

Harrison responded before I could. "Maybe, maybe not. Clearly, something is going on. I say we wait a day or two, then come back to check on our friend here. If he's better, he may be able to tell us more."

"I don't think he's delusional," I said.

Wolf shook his head. "Whatever the case, I don't think you'll be talking to this gentleman again. Have you ever seen anyone with consumption at the end? That poor soul doesn't have long."

I climbed up into the seat, looking back at the cold, dark house. Pity welled up inside of me for the officer. "I'll send Dr. Miller over," I said, more to myself than anyone else. At least the doctor could give the officer something to ease his discomfort.

We drove on in silence. The man's words continued to nag at me. I still didn't know the officer's name. There was more going on, despite what Wolf thought. Whether it was all connected was a different matter.

"We should head to the lab. We haven't been there all day." Harrison broke into my thoughts.

Wolf agreed, saying Mr. Tesla had asked for his help laying wires for a new experiment. "Hopefully, nothing else has happened to make him want to pack up," Wolf mused.

We went back to the lab, Willow, small for her breed, riding in my lap. She enjoyed the cold air blowing in our faces, her mouth open as if she could swallow the freshness. I couldn't enjoy anything. All I could do was think about the officer, about what had happened at his house. How could we possibly wait another couple of days? Tesla was clear. He wanted answers quickly, or he would be leaving us behind.

Harrison reined in Rex inside Tesla's fenced area. The big horse whinnied, chomping at his bit. He and I seem to be in accord. I shifted my feet but remained seated, my gaze glued to the lab door. I didn't want to go inside. There was nothing to report to Mr. Tesla. I thought over the events of the day, hoping to scrape something useful together in order to justify what we did. I tasted metal, realizing I'd been gnawing on my lip.

Willow squirmed in my lap, ready to be released to chase magpies through the field.

A hand on mine made me jump. "You okay, Cora? You're not worried about getting sick, are you? He didn't cough near us." Harrison was trying to reassure me of something that wasn't on my mind.

I glanced down at his hand lingering on my arm. His touch was warm, even through the layers of my coat and dress. For a moment, I thought how hot his touch would be on my bare skin, and my face warmed up with what I was sure was a deep flush.

"I'm not worried about that," I said, flinging my arm up to dislodge Harrison's hand. "I'm worried about not having any useful information for Mr. Tesla."

I handed Willow off to Wolf, who'd been waiting patiently for her next to the buggy. The second her feet hit the ground, she took off with a ripple of fur. I envied her ease of mind and joyful spirit.

"I think we need to face facts. There isn't anything to discover." Harrison shuffled his feet, perhaps annoyed that I kept rejecting his touch.

I continued watching Willow as she sent birds squawking into the air. "I'm not sure. There's something I can't quite figure out." I chewed on my lip as I climbed down.

Harrison was next to me in a flash, his arm offered for support. "It's a little wet. We all know how accident-prone you are."

"Me? I seem to recall someone else ending up on their backside in the snow."

"That's only because it was so dark," he grumbled, his arm never wavering.

I gave in, looping my wrist under his arm. Harrison gave a tug, pulling me in a little closer than I would have liked. I looked up, about to protest our proximity, and found he was grinning from ear to ear.

Everything in me wanted to return that smile. I refused to allow my face to give in. Instead, I straightened my shoulders, moving a step away, but continued to hold his arm.

Harrison chuckled, his eyes never leaving my face. "You know, it's okay to like me, Cora."

I could feel the heat, once again, rush to my face. "Stop

being ridiculous and let's walk."

As I moved forward, pulling Harrison along with me, my gaze swept the area to the left of the lab. Smoke was billowing out of a metal can. "What is Tesla burning?" I asked.

"Scraps, old paper, who knows."

I came to an abrupt halt. A thought I had been trying to grasp earlier unlocked in my brain as I watched flakes of ash fall to the ground around the barrel. "Ashes," I whispered.

"What's that?" Harrison asked, tugging a bit on my arm.

I pulled my arm free, whirling around to face him. "Ashes. Why did we not see it before? The gloved devil with the cigarette is real." I pulled the handkerchief from my pocket, revealing the butt of a cigarette. "I was so distressed by the police officer's condition that I forgot this was with us all along. Our first piece of hard evidence."

CHAPTER ELEVEN

The cigarette butt lolled in the handkerchief. At least my skin was protected from the foul-smelling stump I now held out for the men to see.

"I found this on the floor of Joe's room. Only he didn't smoke. Harrison, Wolf, tell me you see it."

Harrison crossed his arms in front of his chest.

Wolf nodded, looking from the burn pile to me. "It does seem strange, I'll grant you. But it could have been left by one of the police officers. This one object doesn't mean anything sinister occurred," he said.

"It's worth checking out, Cora. Good job." Harrison smiled. He took the handkerchief from me and held it up for a closer look. "Ogden Gold is the brand. These are not cheap. An everyday police officer wouldn't smoke these. Neither would Joe Williams. These are the brand of a fancy gentleman, *maybe* the captain, but that's a big maybe."

Glass and metal crashed to the floor inside the lab. Wolf bolted ahead of us. Harrison and I gaped at each other before running after him. I jumped all three stairs at once, running into the back of Wolf, who stood blocking the way.

As I peered over his shoulder, I saw Tesla with his head in his hands, stumbling near a table he had apparently overturned. Wolf was frozen to his spot. I moved him to the side and rushed toward Tesla. "Can I help you, sir? Is it your head?" I tried to speak softly, unsure of what was happening.

"I need a chair," he whispered.

I shot a look back to Wolf, who finally moved, then turned to put a gentle hand on Tesla's arm. "It's coming. Be still for one moment."

Glass crunched under Wolf's feet as he sat a folding chair behind our boss. "Here, sir." Wolf reached out a hand to guide Tesla back toward the chair.

Harrison appeared at my elbow with a glass of water.

"Do we need to call a doctor?" I eased the glass into Tesla's hand.

"No, no. It's passing now." He raised his head, eyes blinking as if to get clear. He took a long drink of water. "I hope you weren't too alarmed. This happens from time to time. Flashes of blinding light. Often when I'm at work, pondering a question, I'll be besieged by these flashes along with a vision of the solution. Today, I was shaken by thoughts of my current predicament." He stopped, drinking the rest of the water in two gulps.

"Did you have a vision?" Harrison asked.

"I did. Although, I must say it makes no sense. I saw flies, dead ones. I don't see a solution in dead flies."

"Flies?" I asked. "That doesn't help us much, I'm sorry to say."

Tesla shook his head. "I rather didn't think it would. What have you three found out? Dare I ask?"

I shuffled my feet. The men all looked to me. I could see Harrison and Wolf wouldn't be much help. "Well …" I began. "We're not sure. There is a policeman who is willing to talk with us, but he's taken ill. I was planning on returning to see him with the doctor in tow."

Tesla crossed his legs, already back to himself. "There's no time like the present, is there, Miss Croft? I do need at least one of the gentlemen to stay with me this evening.

Enough time has been wasted."

The thought of being alone with Harrison caused my stomach to quiver. Before any decisions could be made, I hastily said, "Wolf, shall we?"

I was sure this would be met with protest, but Harrison remained silent. Wolf looked at Harrison, then back at me. "Sure, Cora."

I couldn't bear to look at Harrison, so I turned on my heel, swiftly making my way to the door. Before I stepped through, I could hear the scrape of broken glass being swept behind me.

Wolf caught up with me outside. "Cora, have you considered how we're going to get around? We came in Harrison's buggy."

My stomach did more than quiver, it dropped. I felt sick. "We can walk …" I ventured.

"Walk? You want to walk to Doc Miller's house, then all the way back to see the cop?"

I closed my eyes against my irritation. I hadn't thought this through one bit. "We need to ask Harrison if we can take his buggy, then come back for him once we've finished," I conceded.

"I suppose that'll be up to me." Wolf rolled his eyes when I didn't say anything. "Wait here," he grumbled.

While I waited, I called back Willow, who continued to maniacally chase the birds, rabbits, and whatever else crossed her path. She came as soon as I called, more trustworthy than most people.

Wolf reemerged, an uncharacteristic smirk on his face. "Let's go," he said as he strode past me.

I plopped Willow in the back, settled beside Wolf, and we were off. Our first stop was Dr. Miller's house on the quaint, tree-lined Tejon Street. The doctor lived in a lovely home, the street here as pretty as my own.

We left Willow fast asleep in the back and went to the house. I pressed the button for the bell and the loud, electric gong made me jump. Isabella would die before she installed one of these electric bells in her home. A young man, lanky and shiny, appeared.

"Good afternoon," I began. "May we speak with Dr. Miller, please?"

The man uttered an inaudible response, standing back for us to enter the foyer. I was taken aback by the appearance of the room and what I could see beyond. In short, the place was a dusty mess. I had never been here myself, as Dr. Miller mostly made house calls, but the surroundings did not seem very clinical. A thick layer of dust could be seen on every surface, a cobweb in one corner. Days-old mud had been tracked along the floor without having been cleaned.

The man again mumbled something I could not make out as he walked down the hall. I glanced at Wolf, who shrugged in response. Unsure of what to do, I followed along. Halfway down the musty-smelling hall, the man opened a door and ushered us inside.

Dr. Miller sat at his desk, the top of his bald head pointing toward us as he scribbled away in a notebook. He reminded me of Tesla, minus the hair. This room, clearly the doctor's office, was a stark contrast to the foyer and hall. Everything was neat and tidy; the furniture, which appeared freshly polished, smelled of lemon and wax.

Dr. Miller jumped almost out of his seat as the door slammed behind us. "Miss Croft," he exclaimed. "My apologies, I didn't see you there. All is well with you, I hope."

I smiled at the town's longtime physician. "Yes, sir. I'm here to ask you to accompany me on a little excursion. There's a policeman who is quite ill. Would you be so kind as to pay him an immediate call? I'm sorry to be so abrupt, but the situation is urgent."

Dr. Miller's chair squeaked as he leaned back. He rubbed his hand over his head as if ruffling his non-existent hair. "Of course, Miss Croft. Allow me to pack my case."

I breathed a sigh of relief and told the good doctor we

would be happy to provide him transportation.

On the way, I related to him the condition in which we found the man earlier.

"I believe Mr. Ward is correct. Classic tuberculosis. There will likely be nothing I can do for him, Miss Croft, other than to help him be comfortable."

I nodded, feeling dismayed. Dr. Miller and I sat in the back with my still-sleeping dog while Wolf drove us to our destination.

"It isn't much of a fall, is it? Seems we've gone straight through to winter," Dr. Miller mused as we drove.

He was right. The trees were mostly bare, prematurely stripped of their falling leaves by the hard snow. The desolation of this time of year often left me a little sad. Winter would be long.

"Strange things seem to be happening since Mr. Tesla arrived in town." Dr. Miller studied the trees that swooshed by.

He had my attention. "What do you mean?"

"Strange weather and such. Have to wonder if it's his contraptions."

I was shocked by Dr. Miller's accusations. Surely, a man as learned as the doctor couldn't believe Tesla was behind the early winter.

"We often have strange weather here, Doctor. Mr. Tesla isn't the problem." I felt oddly protective of Tesla, although I hardly knew him myself. I understood even less of his experiments. However, what little I knew, it didn't stand to reason that he could change the weather.

We reached our destination shortly. The home was in no way changed, except for a filmy fog that hung about the roof, which the shining sun made it feel out of place and unnatural. A chill crept down my back.

Dr. Miller cleared his throat. "My young friends, you should wait here. I'll be out presently." He climbed down from the buggy.

I needed to accompany the doctor if I was to find out more about what was going on. "I insist on going inside, Doctor. This gentleman is a good friend, and I could prove useful as an assistant." I didn't wait for him to respond. Instead, I hopped from the buggy with a light step. *Please don't ask me the man's name.*

Dr. Miller began to protest but I held up a hand. "I'm quite fine, Doctor. Please lead the way."

Dr. Miller shot a look to Wolf, who shrugged. The doctor grumbled by way of response and made his way to the house. He rapped on the door with me right behind him. A cold wind swept over us, raising gooseflesh on the back of my neck. I shivered.

There was no answer. The two of us stood in silence as we stared at the door, willing it to open. Dr. Miller knocked again.

"Perhaps he took himself to the hospital," I mused.

"Perhaps," the doctor mumbled. "He could be unconscious. We should check."

Dread swept over me. Dr. Miller reached out to give the knob a turn. There was a click as the door opened without protest. The doctor pushed it open, stuck to his spot on the front step.

A smell, rank and metallic, assaulted my senses. My hand flew to cover my mouth and nose.

"Oh, dear," said Dr. Miller. "Miss Croft, you need to wait for me at the buggy." He stepped tentatively inside.

The small front room was tidy with nothing amiss. Plain furnishings were neatly polished, cushions on the divan carefully plumped. I watched Dr. Miller step into the center of the room, look around, and call out, "Hello." There was no answer. Neither of us was expecting one.

My breath came and went too rapidly. I gripped the side of the door frame, fearful I would be sick. The smell was overpowering. Still, I couldn't walk away. The doctor went to the closed door at the back of the main room. He knocked, waited a moment, and then pushed the door open.

Dr. Miller sucked in his breath as he took a step back.

Unable to help myself, I dashed to his side. The sight I beheld was beyond reasonable explanation. The man lay on his face in a pool of sick and blood. I'd never seen so much blood. He and the floor were covered in it. My face twisted in horror.

"Cora, run for the captain. Now." Dr. Miller's face was ghost white, a mirror, I was sure, of my own.

I stumbled back, finally ready to do as the doctor asked. I bolted from the house. My body doubled over halfway down the walk. I held my stomach, willing myself not to vomit. I gulped deep breaths of fresh, cold air; the best medicine there was for my unease.

"Cora, what is it?" Wolf stood over me immediately, his hand gently on my back.

"We have to get the captain, Wolf. Now."

CHAPTER TWELVE

Almost two hours elapsed from the time Captain King was found and brought to the little house on Bijou Street. Along with the darkness, a new chill emerged. The smell of snow gathering in the clouds made everything feel more ominous. We were freezing, but I couldn't leave.

No matter how Wolf and Harrison pushed and pulled, I refused to budge.

"We have to get you home, Cora," Wolf groaned. He had returned to the lab to pick up Harrison while I waited behind, perched awkwardly on the walk in front of the house. They were both here now, Wolf trying everything in his power to get me in the buggy while Harrison chewed silently on a fingernail.

"I have to know what happened. You can both leave if you wish." My feet were sore from standing in place, and I was tired, but I had to know.

"I can tell you what happened, Cora. The man died of consumption, plain and simple," Wolf said behind me.

I turned to him, an incredulous look on my face. "You wouldn't say that if you saw what I did. This was something else, something unnatural."

I looked at Harrison, who continued to gnaw at his

finger. I pulled his hand from his mouth. "Stop that. Don't you both think it's a little too coincidental? This man wants to tell us something, something obviously secret, then hours later he dies." The men remained silent.

Finally, after a moment, Harrison said, "We're in over our heads, Cora. I believe you. Something sinister is going on. The thing is, if we're not careful, we could be next. This isn't a game."

I shoved my cold hands in my pockets, fixing Harrison in a glare I was sure could be lethal. "I never said this was a game. I'm not afraid, Harrison Byrne. What I am is determined. Determined to find out as much as I can. Maybe it's foolish to get involved, but I can't just leave this."

Wolf shuffled his feet. "What do you suggest we do, Detective Cora?"

"Keep digging. One of us needs to get in that room and see what we can find." I looked at Harrison as his eyes went wide. "Harrison, why don't you go offer to help inside? Tell them Wolf and I have gone to get coffee and sandwiches."

Harrison looked at the house, his mouth pulled into a grimace. "Why me?"

"You're the most likely to be admitted for several reasons. Your dad's a cop, for one. Go on," I prodded. "You'll be fine. Try to find out what the doctor thinks caused the death and look around for anything that could be a clue."

Harrison closed his eyes, running a hand across his face. "If I come down with some horrible disease, Cora, I'll never forgive you."

I smiled, patting him on the arm. Before Harrison could protest further, I sped toward the buggy, Wolf pulling behind me.

"And where are we going then?" Wolf asked.

"Mr. Hill is close. We'll go there for coffee and food."

The hour was late, and I feared my teacher and his wife would be in bed, but as luck would have it, Mr. Hill opened the door, his glasses perched on his head, an open book in his hand. "Cora, it's awfully late. Are you all right?"

"I am. I'm so sorry to disturb you at this hour, Mr. Hill. There's been a rather gruesome death not far from here, and we've offered to take coffee and sandwiches to the officers and Dr. Miller."

Mr. Hill could not have looked more shocked had I slapped him in the face. He blinked hard, his eyes shut tight for a beat of several seconds, then recovered himself and invited us in. "I'm not going to ask why you're involved, Cora. But I will ask who the poor victim is." Mr. Hill spoke, half-turned as he walked toward the kitchen.

"A young police officer, sir. He was a sort of ... acquaintance."

"I see. How tragic. Well, Mrs. Hill has taken herself to bed. I can make the coffee if you and Mr. Ward, I believe it is, make the sandwiches."

"How rude of me. Yes, this is Marshall Ward. Marshall, my favorite teacher, Mr. Hill."

Mr. Hill told us where to find the bread, cheese, and leftover ham. Wolf and I went to work, sliced bread and ham piled up between us.

With a loaf of bread in one hand and a large knife in the other, I decided to relate what occurred this afternoon with the now-deceased officer. Mr. Hill faced away from us, dropping scoops of measured coffee grounds into his kettle. "Actually, sir. I'd love to tell you a shortened version of events. Your insight would be invaluable."

Mr. Hill set the kettle on the burner and turned back to us. "Continue, Cora. I'm all ears."

I sliced more bread as I related to Mr. Hill our suspicions over Joe Williams's death and Tesla's documents. "This police officer seemed to have information regarding Joe's death. When we arrived at his home, he was horribly ill. By the time we returned with Dr. Miller, he was gone. I've never seen anything like it." I told Mr. Hill of the scene I witnessed in the bedroom.

The look on Mr. Hill's face made me question all I had

said. I could only hope he wouldn't tell Isabella. Mr. Hill's eyes were wide, his chin cupped in his hands as he relaxed against the counter. "You should not be involved in this, Cora. How many people have told you this already?"

"A few, sir."

"I don't like it one bit. It sounds to me as if this officer could have been poisoned. This is a dangerous game. One better left to the police force."

My gaze shifted back to the assembly line of sandwiches. "I understand, Mr. Hill. And you're correct. This is better left to the police."

"Good. I'm glad we're in agreement." Mr. Hill stuffed the sandwiches wrapped in butcher paper inside a large picnic basket and handed it to me. He then took a dish towel, which he used to wrap around the handle of the kettle filled with steaming hot, black coffee. This, he handed to Wolf.

"Careful not to scald yourselves. I can't give you any cups. Mine would be the next gruesome death if I did."

I smiled. "Don't worry, I'm sure we'll find some back at the man's home. Thank you so much, Mr. Hill. You'll find your basket and kettle on the back porch by morning."

"I suppose you wouldn't listen to an old man who told you two to be careful. But, be careful, anyway."

We were back at the house in less than an hour. Three officers milled about in front of a police wagon, pulled by two horses. I didn't see Harrison's father. It was possible he was working inside, or not even here. Wolf and I strode toward the officers, walking with more confidence than we felt.

"Are we going to step aside then, Bird? As Mr. Hill advised?"

"All I said was this was better left to the police. But the police are compromised." It was best to march forward than make eye contact with Wolf.

The men stopped talking. One of them shuffled toward us, his hand up to keep us from getting closer.

I smiled brightly, exuding all the charm I could muster. "Good evening, gentlemen. We're working with Dr. Miller. Would you like some hot coffee and sandwiches?"

The man's expression changed, and I knew we were in. "Can't say no to that," he said.

"Marshall will pass out the sandwiches while I go inside to fetch some cups." I kept my smile in place as I moved around the officers.

"We can't allow you inside, Miss. It's a mess."

"The only mess is in the bedroom. I've already been inside with Dr. Miller, so no need to worry." I turned, hoping to imply I didn't need their permission, and went to the door.

I set the kettle down on the small step and went inside. The front room was unchanged. An officer stood with his back toward me, blocking my view into the bedroom. Noise from the chatter inside drowned out any sound my entrance made. I softly pulled the front door closed behind me, then tiptoed through to the kitchen. I hoped the hinges on this door were as silent as the one I just came through. They were.

Once I was in the kitchen, an odor not of sickness but old food assaulted me. Although not nearly as strong as the bedroom, the smell was enough to warrant a hand over my nose.

A bowl of half-eaten congealed stew sat on the butcher block countertop. The soup was the source of the smell. This must have been the meal he was consuming as he had fallen ill. His lunch, perhaps. I dared not touch it but bent down to take a whiff. Cold meat and potatoes. The stew looked normal enough.

I poked around, peering into cabinets and drawers. Nothing to be found. What I needed to do was get back in the bedroom. Surely, there was no way to do that unless we came back later to look around. May as well add one more break-in to our recent list of crimes.

I was about to gather a few mugs from the open shelf when I took notice of the back door. Were my eyes playing tricks on me or was the wood near the handle splintered? I went closer to inspect, running my hand along the door frame. A fragment of wood came off on my fingertip.

It appeared as if I wasn't the first to think of breaking into this home. I took a peek outside into the darkness. The side area was hidden well by two oak trees. These would block the view of the neighboring house, obscuring anyone who entered or left. The deserted night gave me a chill of terror. I ducked my head back inside the kitchen.

As I did so, a flash of white caught my eye. Stuck into a sharp shard of fractured wood was a piece of fabric. I pulled it loose, rolling it between my thumb and middle finger. The fabric was a fine silk, clearly expensive. It could have come from the cuff of a shirt, a dress, or a … glove.

The slip of silk fell from my fingers. I closed the door, acutely aware someone could be watching me. My hand stayed pressed against the wood, breath hitched. Harrison was right; we had put ourselves in danger, and for what, I wasn't sure now. I placed my hand over my staggering heartbeat, willing it back into a normal rhythm.

We were doing this for a reason, to help Mr. Tesla. We were too late to help Joe and the officer, but we could keep anyone else from getting hurt, since the police didn't seem able or interested. Perhaps they would now, as they'd lost one of their own. Although, with Joe, it seemed they knew. This man did at any rate and possibly covered it up.

My suspicion was now this; the dead man was one of the two officers to first inspect the room where Joe was murdered. Who was the second? The man I ran to for help? Harrison's father? The second man could be anyone. He could also be in danger.

At that moment, I made a rash decision. I snapped up the fragment of silk, jamming it into the same pocket that held the handkerchief-wrapped cigarette. I grabbed four cups and went quietly out the way I came.

"Here you are, gentlemen." I passed the cups to the three officers and one to Wolf, who had a strange look on his face. The officers began munching on their sandwiches within seconds.

"What?" I mouthed at Wolf. He shook his head.

I filled the men's cups from the still-warm kettle, then set it back on the stoop. Wolf followed me.

"What is it?" I whispered, hoping we were far enough away to be out of earshot.

Wolf turned his back on the men. "Dr. Miller thinks this man was poisoned, Cora."

"Well, that is what Mr. Hill thought from my description."

"Yes, but to hear the doc say it is different somehow. I'm scared, Bird. You don't seem bothered."

"I am and I'm not. I told you something unnatural happened in there." I couldn't tell Wolf about the silk until we were clear of the police. I couldn't risk one of them hearing us. "I don't think there's much more we can do here until everyone leaves. As soon as Harrison comes out, we'll pretend to go home."

Wolf sucked in his breath, his head shaking from side to side. "Cora …" he began.

"Not now. You can admonish me later. Let's get through these next minutes, then get clear of this place."

Wolf gritted his teeth, handing me his coffee. "I'll wait in the buggy."

By the time Harrison came out, the three officers had polished off all the coffee and sandwiches. The poor souls working inside the nightmare of the bedroom were out of luck. I didn't think we should hang around any longer, so I handed the basket and kettle to Harrison and motioned toward the buggy.

No one was paying us any mind as they were loading the body of the deceased into the back of the wagon. Harrison's eyes were drawn, his hands shook, and he smelled faintly of the sick room.

"Are you all right?" I asked once we were on our way back to Mr. Hill's.

"No, Cora. Not especially. I had to move the body from side to side so Dr. Miller and the captain could look all around it. It was all I could do not to lose the contents of my own stomach. Thank goodness my dad wasn't there."

"I'm sorry, Harrison. Thank you for going in." I wanted to ask if he saw anything or found out any more information but thought it best to wait a moment or two. I bit my lip, squirming in my seat.

"The only reason they let me in was because the grunts hadn't arrived yet, and neither the captain nor his assistant would touch the body."

"You were so brave." I patted his hand.

Harrison rolled his eyes. "I'll put you out of your misery. I'm sure you already know some of it. Dr. Miller says the man was poisoned, likely with something called Spanish fly. That was the only useful thing I learned in that room."

"What on earth is Spanish fly?" asked Wolf from the driver's box.

"According to Dr. Miller, it's known mostly as being an aphrodisiac but can cause the exact symptoms the officer— Daniel McAdams, was his name—was exhibiting. Apparently, the doctor had seen this kind of thing before, overseas." Harrison paused, looking uncomfortable.

I blushed, turning my head away.

"That doesn't make sense." Wolf made a strange sound.

"It didn't make sense to them, either. They thought the man must have been fooling around with the substance and ingested too much. But it makes sense to me. Spanish fly is deadly, remarkably so. I read an article about it once. Anyway, the doctor and captain were going on like this death was an accident. We know better, don't we?"

I thought of the cups I handed to the officers. They seemed to be clean. My stomach lurched. Then I remembered what the man had said. He started to feel ill after eating his lunch. The stew still sitting on the counter was poisoned.

"If they're already convinced the death was an accident, then they may overlook the back door being forced."

"The back door was forced?" Harrison looked at me, his eyes clearing up.

"It was. And, I found this." I pulled the piece of silk from my pocket, holding it up in the moonlight.

CHAPTER THIRTEEN

"Your pockets contain endless amounts of evidence. Anything else you want to show us?" Harrison eyed me through narrow slits.

"Not at the moment."

"I don't believe we'll learn anything by going back to that room," Harrison said, a shudder running down his arms. "Not only can I not handle the smell again, but after the doc and captain were finished with me, I looked around. There was nothing in the room except a bedside table. No books, scraps of paper, or anything else. Where did you get the coffee and sandwiches, by the way?"

"From Mr. Hill. He was the closest person I could think of who would help us without too many questions."

Harrison shifted in his seat. "Cora, I've heard some things about Mr. Hill. You shouldn't have taken anything from him."

I turned toward Harrison, bewildered by what he could mean. "What things?" Part of me was a little jealous Harrison may know more about my favorite teacher than I did.

He shrugged. "Just that he may have to quit teaching because of his legs, his knees or something. The rumor is, and I emphasize the word rumor, without his job, he and Mrs. Hill may lose their house."

I was astounded that I hadn't heard this. Mr. Hill had mentioned not being able to stand for long periods. Why hadn't he told me the situation was much worse? Poor Mr. Hill, and I had gone to his house and taken his coffee and food.

"Do you have any coins, Harrison? I'll pay you back. I want to leave them in the basket."

Harrison shook his head. "Don't you dare, Cora. To do so would be an insult to Mr. Hill. Just let it be."

Harrison was right. My gut twisted. What could I do to help my teacher that wouldn't look like charity? This question was mentally added to the ever-growing list of problems I now faced.

After leaving Mr. Hill's items on the back porch, I rejoined Wolf and Harrison in the buggy. The hour was quite late, the air frigid, and the dark sky was spitting flakes of fluffy, white snow. Harrison examined the fragment of silk while Wolf held up a match.

"This could be from anything. However, it does fit with the whole gloved-fiend thing. I guess all we need to do is examine every set of gloves in Colorado Springs. Should be easy enough." Harrison was being sarcastic, but he wasn't wrong. This seemed an impossible task. He handed me the piece of material and leaned back against the seat.

Wolf blew out the match. "Whatever we decide to do next, we all need to get home and get some sleep."

"Agreed," Harrison and I said in unison.

As much as I wanted to keep going, I was exhausted. Sitting on the street as we were in the middle of a freezing night was in no way practical.

As Wolf drove us back to my house, a thought occurred to me. "Maxwell Priest worked with Thomas Edison once, didn't he?"

Harrison looked toward me. "Yes, I believe so. Are you thinking he could be a suspect?"

"Maybe. I know him socially, as you know. He's been acting quite odd lately. He also suggested my mother …" I trailed off as I realized this was something I didn't want to touch on right now.

"Your mother?" Harrison prompted.

"Nothing, I was thinking of something else. But he smokes. He also has a penchant for fine silk shirts and gloves. Let's keep Mr. Priest in our thoughts. Tomorrow, we'll reconvene to discuss where to go from here." I yawned. Tomorrow. Something was happening tomorrow. "Oh, no," I groaned. "Tomorrow night is Dove's engagement party. I forgot to go with her to the dressmakers."

Harrison laughed, a little too loudly. "If only we all had such problems." He jumped from the buggy, offering me his hand. "Don't worry, Cora. I'm sure you'll find something to wear."

"Don't patronize me, Harrison Byrne; I'm not in the mood." I refused his hand and climbed down on my own. I turned back to scoop up my dog, who was as done with this day as I was. Willow sprinted toward the door. Her last burst of energy for the day.

"I was kidding, Cora," he called after me. "We'll reconvene the day after tomorrow, then? Let's meet at the park at noon."

I was too tired and annoyed to respond. I raised my hand as I walked, hoping that would suffice as a yes. I felt a bit at a stand-still. How much did we really know at this point? It didn't feel like a lot. Having the day to think on the case seemed a good idea. Maybe what we all needed was to take a step back. Perhaps the day would give us time to reflect on what had happened to create a more solid plan going forward.

All I could think about right now was peeling myself out of my clothes, scrubbing my skin until it was bright pink, and then collapsing into my bed. Before I did any of that, I took the handkerchief-wrapped cigarette and the scrap of silk and shoved them in the back drawer of my writing desk.

A wet tongue startled me awake. "Willow, yuck." I giggled, pulling the dog under the blankets for a snuggle.

A dip in the bed near my feet made me jump. "Mother, good morning."

"Morning was hours ago, Cora. Where were you so late last night? I saw Wolf and the Byrne boy drop you from my window."

The Byrne boy? I decided not to comment. "We were at the experimental station, Mother. Where do you think we'd be? Mr. Tesla doesn't keep banker's hours."

She squeezed her lips together.

"Look, Mother. Everything is fine. Let's talk about it this evening. Do you know what you're wearing?" My words came out in a rush as a sort of diversion away from Tesla and my evening out with two young men.

Mother rose from the bed, then moved toward the window. "It hardly matters what I'll be wearing." She glanced over her shoulder. "I see you haven't opened the box Dove sent over."

Isabella pulled open the curtains. A stream of sunlight fell into the room, waking everything up. I hadn't noticed Dove's box the night before.

I pulled on my dressing gown as I reluctantly exited my warm bed. Marsh had been in to light the fire before I woke. Had she not, the room would have been ice cold. I was eternally grateful for Marsh. Exhaustion had overtaken me the night before. I hadn't even bathed as I wished to do.

"How do you find Mr. Tesla? Have you had many conversations with him?" Mother spoke as I reached the foot of the bed.

"What do you mean? He's very much himself—very singular, if that's what you want to know. And, no, we haven't conversed much." Mother's inquiry struck me as odd. Of course, I would have conversations with Tesla. One usually spoke to their employer. I shook off the strange manner of discourse and focused on what lay before me.

The large white box with the blue silk ribbon sat on the bench at the foot of my bed. The ribbon slipped to the floor as I pulled it off. Inside was a silk gown in the most gorgeous color I had ever seen.

"Oh, Dove," I said aloud.

The gown I pulled from the box had no equal. The bodice was a lapis-blue silk with sleeves that would lie delicately on the edge of my shoulders. The front of the skirt and the back of the bustle were an emerald-green silk. Side panels of the lapis blue peeked out from the folds of green, which all fell in one column to the floor.

"The colors of your favorite bird. You'll look beautiful in that, Cora." Mother moved alongside me, taking the dress from my hands to splay out on the bed.

Mother was correct about the colors. These were the hues of a peacock combined into one artful gown. After being stood up by me, Dove used my measurements already on the books. She had done well. The gown was gorgeous.

"I'll have to pay her back." I opened my wardrobe and selected a free hanger.

Mother left me to my machinations. I begged fatigue and took luncheon in my room. There wasn't much time to consider the events of yesterday. I wasn't bothered too much, as I needed a break from the all-too-harsh reality of death and intrigue. There was only one thing I could think to do before dressing. At my desk, I pulled out ink, quill, and paper. My purpose was to think of anyone who may benefit from Mr. Tesla's ideas. I realized quickly how little I knew of the man. Only one person came to mind. I wrote the name on the paper, folded it, and placed it in the drawer.

Society balls were not usually my favorite pastime. This evening, however, should be fun. It would be nice to spend time with my friend in celebration of her happiness.

A few hours later, I was dressed, perfumed, and coiffed. Marsh was a master of the modern hairstyle. Most of my hair was coiled onto the back of my head in a beautiful spiral, pinned in place with three diamond-studded pins. A few tendrils were left to artfully spiral down my neck and over my shoulder. A single feather dyed a deep blue peeked out over my right ear, the illusion of the peacock complete.

My grandmother's diamond necklace and matching earbobs were the final touches. Mother and I draped our black velvet capes over our shoulders, careful not to crumple our fine silks, as we walked out to the covered chaise.

I shivered in the back seat, careful to not let my teeth chatter. Our thin gowns provided little insulation for the cold ride ahead. Mother had to be as cold as I was, yet she showed no sign. She insisted we not cover our laps with the heavy fur blanket, to keep our dresses as wrinkle-free as possible.

I could not continue to freeze for another thirty minutes until our arrival at Glen Eyrie, so I pulled the fur from the seat across from us onto my lap. Mother eyed me without turning her head. She could be as disappointed as she wanted in my fortitude, but I could stand the cold no longer.

After what seemed like an hour, we were finally making our way through the grand gate of Glen Eyrie. This was the loveliest estate in Colorado Springs. The grounds were expansive with rolling hills, walking paths, gardens, fountains, and trees of all kinds. No matter how many times I attended parties here, I still felt a little thrill driving in.

The grandness of the affair was evident as soon as we pulled up. Chaises were lined up and down the drive, dropping off splendidly dressed men and women. The grounds were aglow with lanterns that cast a most romantic light. The clapboard house itself was not as impressive as the surrounding landscape, but it was as bright and inviting as the lawn. Every window of the twenty-room home was alight with a warm glow.

General Palmer's beloved wife, Queen, died five years ago in England. Currently, the general occupied Glen Eyrie with his three daughters. He was working on plans to extensively renovate. Dove said the general dreamed of creating a large stone castle with over sixty rooms. If the building ever came to fruition, I had no doubt it would be magical.

Mother and I joined the line of people making their way to the house. The inside was sure to be crammed with bodies all swishing around in their fine silks. Fires burning in pits around the front of the property led me to believe General Palmer likely expected some people to remain outside, or at least he hoped they would.

The moment we crossed the threshold, my wrap was taken by an overworked-looking little man. I thought I may keep it, but the interior of the home was hot, stifling even.

"Cora, there you are. If I didn't love you dearly, I may be quite irritated with your absence these last few days." The sea of guests parted naturally for Dove. "You look exquisite. I knew those colors would suit you." Dove clasped my hands in hers, kissing me on both cheeks.

She was one to talk. My friend was, without a doubt, the belle of the ball. Her skin glowed with warmth and happiness, her cheeks and lips the perfect shade of pink. Dove's gown of ice-blue silk clung to her well-balanced figure with perfection. Diamonds I had never seen her wear dripped from her ears and neck. Gifts, I suspected from her fiancé. There was a slight shadow in her eyes. No doubt Dove had worn herself out with the preparations.

In one hand, she swished a delicate lace fan, with her other, she took hold of my elbow, guiding me further into the room. I looked back for Isabella, but she was lost in the sea of high society.

The furniture had been cleared from the rooms, allowing space for more people. The farther we walked into the din, the fainter I felt. We finally came to a stop in the dining room, free of its enormous oak table and chairs.

A delicious breeze from the open windows grazed my bare arms, cooling me down a good bit. Timothy Sharp stood in the center of the room, his back to us as we approached. He was a tall man with a formidable bearing. The small crowd of people gathered around him seemed enthralled by whatever he was saying.

A tray of champagne floated by. After placing her fan under her arm, Dove smoothly lifted off two glasses, passing one to me. She placed a light hand on her fiancé's back, stopping his speech in its tracks. Timothy turned around with the grace of a dancer, Dove fixed in his gaze.

"My love," he said with a half bow to a giggling Dove. "And, Miss Croft. How splendid to see you again." Timothy scooped up my hand, planting a feathery light kiss on the back of my fingers.

I wanted to like him, really, I did. There was no reason why I should not. He had a spotless reputation, was well-respected, and treated Dove exactly as she deserved. If only he wasn't taking her away so abruptly. The courtship, the engagement, it was all happening too fast. Therefore, I couldn't help but feel some disdain for him. No matter how unwarranted.

Timothy turned back to his audience to continue his performance. Dove pulled me next to her, and we were absorbed in the group. I sipped at my champagne, trying with all my might to affect an interest in what Timothy was saying. Try as I might, I could not drum up any interest in railroads.

My mind began to wander back to Harrison, Tesla, and our mystery. Harrison had proved rather helpful. More than helpful, if I was being honest. Wolf, I had known for many years, and his willingness to help, albeit a little reluctant, was no surprise. He wasn't thrilled to be involved, but I knew he wanted to look out for me. That was what drove him to help.

Harrison, on the other hand, I hardly knew. Yet, he was eager, more than eager at times, to jump into situations that were dangerous. I told myself this was due to his interest in helping Mr. Tesla. But, if I were being honest, I didn't get the feeling that Harrison was terribly concerned if Tesla remained or left town.

"Cora, are you unwell?" Dove startled me out of my thoughts with a question I seemed to have been asked a lot lately. She placed a cool hand on my back. How could she be so cool when the room was so blasted hot?

"I'm fine," I lied, realizing my face was moist and my breathing shallow.

"We're going outside." Dove took my champagne glass and handed both mine and hers to a lady standing nearby.

She then took me by the arms, steered me around and toward the back door. The moment the cold, night air swept across my face, I felt a hundred times better. I braced my hands against the stone half wall, which wound around the porch, and breathed in deeply.

"Goodness, let me get you some water."

"No, wait. I'm fine, don't leave." I was feeling much better already. Being left alone in the dark did not appeal. "I was overheated, that's all."

Dove placed a hand on my forehead, concern in her eyes. I could barely make her out by the light from the house.

"You better not be getting sick, Cora Croft. You've been running yourself ragged. I demand to know what you've been up to."

I related the last few days to my friend, who stood in front of me with her hand over her mouth. It only took me a matter of minutes to spew forth all I had entangled myself in.

"I don't know how I feel about this, Cora. This really doesn't sound like something you should be involved with." Dove had stepped back in her shock. It was impossible to read her face in the shadows.

I was beginning to shiver. "Let's go back inside. I don't want you to come down with an illness at your engagement party."

"Neither do I. And so close to the wedding."

I stopped in my tracks. "What do you mean? Surely, it isn't all that soon."

Dove stepped into the light with pursed lips. "Cora, really. I understand you've been busy, but I did leave you a note. I left it on your bedside table yesterday when I delivered the dress. I wanted to tell you in person, but I'd no idea when I would catch you, and the back room of that horrible lab didn't seem like the right place. Timothy needs to settle in Denver as soon as possible. The wedding is in three weeks."

CHAPTER FOURTEEN

"Three weeks?" I almost gagged on the words. Dove barely knew this man. How could she be so certain he was right for her? When I looked at Timothy Sharp, all I felt was irritation. He was vapid, vain, and arrogant.

Dove had real depth and a good heart. I didn't see how she could be happy with him. How to communicate all this to my friend without hurting her? I took a breath before responding. "Three weeks is so soon, Dove. Are you sure you're ready? This is a big change."

Dove placed her cold hand on my arm, gently pushing me toward the door. "It's the biggest change of my life, Cora. I'm ready for it, I really am." She smiled sweetly, teeth beginning to chatter.

I would have to hold on to my thoughts about her union, for now, and think better how to approach this. A party was no place for an argument, so I allowed her to nudge me inside. The change in temperature from the terrace to the back hall was extreme. There seemed to be no middle ground. I went weak in the knees, then adjusted.

I followed Dove back to where her fiancé was still holding court. I felt like a petulant child. All I wanted to do was go home and sleep. That is, until Tesla's name fell from

Timothy Sharp's lips.

"Yes, I suppose the man is a genius," he said. "But, so disorganized. A mess, really. I, for one, won't be surprised if he leaves Colorado having learned nothing."

"How would you know?" I snapped. Every face in the room turned toward me. Heat blazed in my cheeks. I hadn't meant to speak out loud. I looked at Dove, whose mouth was hanging all the way open, an odd look in her eye.

Timothy Sharp howled a loud, pompous guffaw. "Of course, Miss Croft has a different opinion. She works for him, after all. Tell us, Cora. How does Tesla get on with his experiments?"

The faces continued to stare at me. Did these people not blink? I swallowed dry, hot air. "Well," I began.

I wanted to tell them all the wonderful things Mr. Tesla had discovered since setting up his lab outside the city. The truth was, even if I hadn't been bound by his confidentiality contract, I had no idea how his experiments were going. I knew, as did the rest of the town, the gist of why he was here—to send signals from Pikes Peak to Paris—but that was all. Had he succeeded? Was he working on anything else besides his telescope and the artificial lightning? Those answers were a mystery. The notes I had typed, which seemed centuries ago, were more vague than detailed, with odd phrases thrown in that had me thinking of secret codes. I could have spoken of the communications from space he spoke of in his letter, but I would never betray Tesla in that way.

I squared my shoulders, raising my face to meet the crowd. "Everyone who works in the experimental station is bound by confidentiality. I'm not allowed to talk about it."

The people around me turned to each other, murmuring in low tones impossible to decipher. My gaze returned to Mr. Sharp. He narrowed his eyes and his mouth turned into a grin I did not like. Oddly, I had the feeling he was sizing me up. But, why?

Without breaking eye contact with me, Timothy Sharp

reached into his pants pocket and pulled forth a gold cigarette case. I felt a shiver run down my spine despite the heat of the room.

"Miss Croft." Mr. Sharp popped open the lid of the case with a flick of his thumb and held the exposed cigarettes toward me.

"Yes, thank you." I didn't smoke but took the offer of a cigarette.

He then offered one to his soon-to-be bride, who shook her head. Dove watched me with wide eyes, surely shocked to see me smoke.

Something about Sharp was nagging at me. Was it just a general loathsomeness or something more? My legs trembled with nerves as I clutched the cigarette between my fingers. "What is it about Mr. Tesla that intrigues you so, Mr. Sharp? You seem overly curious about what goes on in his lab. Are you aware someone has been attempting to steal from him?" I studied Sharp's face as I spoke. There could have been a slight twitch of the eyelids, but the movement was gone before I could fully register it. Perhaps this was too much. I didn't want to upset Dove.

"Merely interested." Sharp indicated the crowd with a sweep of his hand. "Who here isn't?" There was a general agreement as the people within earshot all murmured their assent.

Mr. Sharp dug into his coat pocket, procuring a book of matches. He struck one, holding it out for me. I was going to have to dissemble for at least one or two puffs. This would take more self-possession than anything else I'd yet done. I placed the cigarette between my lips, leaned forward, and touched the end to the lit match. I inhaled, paper and tobacco crackling in the flame.

It took every ounce of willpower I possessed not to choke on the vile smoke that invaded my lungs. I swallowed it down, smoke pouring from my nostrils on the exhalation. Timothy Sharp continued to watch me.

"If you'll excuse me," I said with the practiced air of a

socialite. "I need to check in with my mother."

Without making eye contact with Dove, I whirled around and walked from the room, the cigarette held aloft between my fingers. As soon as I was clear of the dining room, I made for the first ashtray I could spy.

General Palmer's study was unoccupied. An empty crystal ashtray rested on the edge of his desk, which I used to stub out the cigarette. I took a fresh handkerchief from my handbag, wrapped it, and pushed it into the bottom.

"Well, Cora. Since when do you smoke, and why are you after Timothy? You know better than anyone that Mr. Priest is the one obsessed with Tesla."

I spun around to find Dove in the doorway. "I only thought I would try it. Now seemed as good a time as any." I prayed she wouldn't see the empty ashtray and wonder what I had done with the cigarette. "And, I'm sorry. I let my words get away from me."

Dove stepped further into the room. I moved in front of the desk, blocking the view to its contents.

"You're acting so strange. I'm worried about you and this nonsense with Mr. Tesla. To insert yourself into those bizarre deaths, smoking. Not to mention out at all hours with Wolf and Harrison Byrne. I wish you would stop taking such risks."

I laughed. "How funny. Dove Mackenzie is telling me to stop taking risks." I hadn't meant to sound so derisive.

Dove's eyes changed from soft and concerned to flashing and narrowed. "What do you mean?"

I bit my lip so hard I tasted blood. My stomach churned from cigarette smoke and nerves. "I'm talking about you and Timothy Sharp. What do you really know about him, Dove? This is all happening a bit fast, isn't it? What's the rush? Why does he need to marry you so quickly?" My rapid-fire questions seemed to hit Dove in the face as she took a step back to steady herself.

"Maybe because he loves me, Cora, and doesn't want to wait. Why does it have to be more complicated than that?

Need I remind you that you're going off to who knows where next year? I've never been anything but supportive of your dreams, Cora. Is it so much to ask you to support mine? Or are mine not grand enough for you?"

I felt as if the wind had been knocked out of me. Dove turned in a swish of silks and bolted out the door.

"Dove—wait." Tears stung my eyes. I collapsed back against the desk. Supporting myself with my hands, I leaned forward, head bowed.

My best friend was right. I wasn't being supportive, and I likely ruined her engagement party. I was only as worried for her as she was for me. This excuse seemed of little consequence as I burst into tears.

"Cora, what on earth?" Mother's arms were around me. "I've been looking everywhere for you."

I wiped snot and tears with the back of my hand. "I don't feel well, Mother. I need to go home."

She felt my forehead with the back of her cool hand. "You're burning up. Come on." She looped an arm around my waist, pulling me along with her as we fought the crowd of people to the front door.

Mother deftly made our excuses as we walked, several people stepping away from the seemingly sick girl. Only I wasn't sick. Although I probably looked deathly ill, I was tired, confused, and if I was being honest, a little heartbroken.

My mouth tasted like ashes. All I wanted to do was get home, clean up, and go to bed. The night was a disaster. I couldn't stand to have Dove mad at me. First thing in the morning, I was resolved to knock on her door with my tail tucked between my legs. For tonight, I needed to retreat.

Mother allowed me silence as we drove home. I closed my eyes, trying to clear my mind. This was a next to impossible task after the events of the last few days. My thoughts were crowded with unpleasant images: the dead body of Joe Williams, his broken attic window, the dead body of the police officer in his blood-covered bedroom, and the crestfallen face of my best friend.

All I had wanted was to work in Mr. Tesla's lab, assisting him with his electrical experiments while learning all I could. Instead, I was traipsing around the city, involving myself in mysterious, dangerous matters, and upsetting my Dove.

By the time Walters pulled up to our house, I could have slept for days if only given the chance. Weariness permeated my bones. I said goodnight to Mother and trudged up the stairs, my head and heart downcast.

Marsh came in to help me undress. "You're home early. Are you unwell? You look flushed."

I held the front of my gown in place as Marsh unbuttoned the back. "Why do people keep asking me that? I'm not physically unwell," I said, staring down at the floor.

Marsh made a grunting sound. "I've been there, Miss. Give it time." She patted my back with a quick motion then went back to unbuttoning. This was the most sentiment Marsh could muster, but it meant the world.

The dull ache that had been throbbing in my head ramped up into a more insistent pounding. By the time Marsh finished helping me out of the peacock-colored dress, I was beginning to see flashes of light. I thought of Tesla. If only my blinding headache would lead me toward a vision of Joe's killer. It wouldn't, of course. All I was likely to receive for my troubles was an upset stomach caused by the terrible pain in my head.

I stumbled across the hall to my mother's room. One hand pressed to my temple, one to my belly as I walked unevenly across the carpet. Mother kept pain tablets in her desk drawer and was very particular about doling them out. She had to be certain that a person was indeed in the throes of a headache and not overreacting. She was cautious of anyone "developing a habit."

My knuckles rapped lightly on the door. Light spilled from underneath the door jamb. She was awake, yet there was no answer. Perhaps she was in her bathroom. I pushed the door open, my determination set on her desk drawer where I knew the tablets were kept. The pounding only increased—I would happily meet her ire.

The drawer was locked. I groaned as my gaze swept around the room. Mother could not abide snooping, but I was desperate. She could yell at me all she wanted tomorrow. Every drawer and miniature door were opened and ransacked until I found the desired object. The small gold key was the most beautiful object I had ever seen.

I turned the key in the lock, sliding the drawer out to reveal the desired bottle. As my fingers grasped the pills, I spied what appeared to be a broken piece of wood toward the back of the compartment. Curiosity got the better of me. I tugged at the partition and my breath caught in my throat. Letters, dozens of them, were jammed into a small hidden recess.

Before I could catch myself, I picked one up and flipped it over in my hand. My mouth fell open. On the front of the letter was written, *To my Isabella—your loving Joe.*

"Cora Croft."

I jumped almost out of my skin, the letter falling from my grasp. Mother rushed toward me, roughly pushing me away from her desk. Her face was red, her eyes flashed fire. "What are you doing? Have you lost leave of your senses?"

"I … I …" I stammered. "I needed the headache tablets. I'm so sorry … my head." I took a step back, ready to flee.

Mother pulled the bottle from the drawer, thrusting it toward me. "Here. Get out."

I grabbed it, running from the room in retreat. Never had I seen my mother so angry. Her voice shook as she choked on the fury so clear in her eyes.

Back in my room, I poured a glass of water with unsure hands. The lid was stubborn, and it took me several hard seconds before the top finally came loose. I went to the bathroom to clean up and rinse my mouth, the still ashy taste of the cigarette present on my tongue. I was too tired, too upset to change into a nightgown, so I slipped under the covers in my dressing gown. My eyes were heavy, my thoughts tangled. I stared up at the ceiling, wondering how I could shut these images out.

The door clicked open. Mother stood at the entrance, a candle burning in a silver candlestick held aloft in her hand.

"Mother, you should be in bed, too. What do you need?" I was tired beyond reason. If Mother was here to continue to chide me for snooping or make some excuse about the letters, I didn't want to hear it. I wouldn't be surprised to see her turn all this to her advantage. Surely, she had something to say about the late hours I was keeping and my involvement with Mr. Tesla. I wasn't in the mood. The look on Isabella's face, glowing from the flame of the candle, told me I didn't have much choice.

I sat up against the headboard to await whatever dire news she held within.

Rather than sit, she continued to stand inside the doorway. "Cora, it came to my attention this evening that you have been involving yourself in the death of Joseph Williams. Given what you just saw, I think now is the best time to discuss this."

My stomach twisted. Who had told her? Dove was the only one who knew. Was she so angry with my behavior that she somehow got to Mother before we left to tell her what I was doing? My head still hurt terribly. I tried to think back on the encounter in General Palmer's study. It was possible Dove ran into Mother before she confronted me, but why would she tell her? My mind felt addled. That scenario didn't make sense. The information must have come from someone else. Who there would have known?

I attempted to keep my face still, not wanting my eyes to betray me. I took a measured breath. "Yes, Mother. I suppose I have. There is a reasonable explanation, though."

At this, she held up her hand.

My mouth snapped shut.

"Whatever reason you think you have doesn't matter. It ends now. I don't know what's gotten into you, Cora. I'm not sure if this has something to do with Mr. Tesla's influence or Harrison Byrne's, but it's now over." She closed her eyes for a moment as if thinking of what to say next.

My mind raced as I tried to think of what I could possibly do or say to get her to understand. She crossed to the bench, perching herself on the edge, one hand still clutching the candlestick.

"There's more." She paused, gaze flitting away. The minutes seemed to stretch out endlessly. When she looked back at me, it seemed an hour had passed. "All during the drive home, I was wondering what I should do about this. Knowing you as I do, you are as stubborn as your father was, I wanted to think longer on how I should address this. But now you've forced my hand."

Mother sighed, her shoulders slumped in a posture of defeat I had never seen from her. "The letters you found are from Joseph Williams. We were … involved. I don't owe you or anyone else an explanation as to why. It's enough to say that I cared for Joe, dearly. I'm a grown woman, and this is all we will say on the matter. You, my dear, are not as grown as you would like to imagine. Not only that, but as you still reside under my roof, you will adhere to my rules. I didn't like you working in that lab from the beginning. Your presence there is now completely out of the question. You have placed yourself in a multitude of dangerous situations. It ends now, as I've said. You needn't argue or attempt to plead your case. This is all we will say. Am I understood?"

Sometime during the epilogue, I had crossed my arms tightly across my chest. I squeezed my hands shut underneath my arms, nails biting into the flesh of my palms. Mother would not tolerate an argument. I knew better. Perhaps she could be swayed in a day or two when her anger subsided. Now, however, she expected nothing less than a yes. I thought of the perfume Harrison smelled on Joe's curtains. It was my mother's. She didn't want me to work with Tesla because she was afraid I could find out. This was the only explanation that made sense. I was bewildered by her. The night she told me about the death in town, she seemed so detached. My mother wasn't a fragile woman, but there hadn't been even a whisper of emotion. What else didn't I know?

As much as it pained me to do so, I muttered, "Yes, Mother."

"Good. Now go to bed, Cora. You look like death." She righted her shoulders into their usual posture as she rose. As soon as she shut my door behind her, I exhaled a long breath, unbidden tears falling from my eyes.

They were swiped angrily away. "No more tears tonight."

CHAPTER FIFTEEN

Sleep was not easily found. I tossed and turned so much Willow jumped from the bed to sleep on the floor, annoyed with my constant movements. All I could think of was my mother with Joe Williams. Isabella was a beautiful woman. As much as I didn't like to think about it, a love affair was not all that shocking. Her choice of man was the shocking thing. He was young. I believed him to be somewhere in his mid-twenties. I pushed my face into my pillow and screamed. This was too much, it was all too much.

A sound somewhere in the dark sent me bolt upright. I sat still in the dark, my gaze darting around the room. Did I imagine the sound? Perhaps my scream had been louder than I intended, and Isabella would throw the door open at any moment, angry with me for rousing her from her bed.

Another sound alerted my attention to the window. A scratch against the pane pushed my heart into my throat. I whipped my head around, and my breath all but stopped. My heart stuttered in my chest. I thought to scream, without the pillow this time.

A head-shaped shadow was silhouetted through the white lace. I cursed myself for not having drawn the heavy velvet curtains. Could whoever it was see inside? I held back the covers, touching my feet silently to the floor. It seemed ridiculous, but I dropped all the way down to my hands and knees. Could the intruder see my shadow as I could see his? I looked back at my dog curled up near the still-warm fireplace. She hadn't budged.

With deliberate slowness, I crawled to the window, staying over to the side. When I was behind the curtain panel, I reached out a shaky hand and ever-so-slightly peeled back the white lace, keeping myself as hidden as possible. A man's head levitated outside.

"Cora." As soon as the head said my name, I realized at once who it was.

Relieved annoyance flooded through me. I stood in a huff, pushing the lace fully out of the way. Harrison Byrne clutched precariously to the trellis alongside my window. I pushed up the pane for him to crawl onto the window seat. He wore the same clothes he had worn all day. I wondered if he had even been home.

The moonlight shone on his auburn hair, his face showing a day's worth of stubble. I realized I was standing in front of him in nothing but a sheer dressing gown. My cheeks flamed as I stepped away to pull a quilt from my bed. This I held in front of me like a shield.

"Why are you climbing the walls of my home and scratching on my window in the middle of the night? What couldn't wait until tomorrow?"

Harrison grinned that infuriating grin. I refused to melt. "I thought, like me, you may be unable to sleep and would be up for some snooping."

I chewed the inside of my lip as I considered this. How much more trouble could I possibly get myself into? "Snooping where?"

"Maxwell Priest has gone to San Francisco on the train. He'll be gone two days, taking his butler and assistant along with him. This means his house will be empty."

I swallowed. "How do you know all this?"

Harrison crossed his legs smugly. "I took him and his

entourage to the depot about an hour ago."

I had to give it to Harrison. This was a good idea. We were lucky to have such an opportunity. One we may never get again. For a second, I couldn't believe how I had changed so much in the span of only a few days. Never had I so much as thought to break the law. Now, I was breaking into people's homes, sneaking out in the middle of the night, and lying to police officers, Isabella, and Mr. Hill.

"Two days gives us plenty of time to go to his house. We don't need to jump the gun," I reasoned. The throbbing in my head had subsided, and I felt well enough for an excursion, but sleepiness continued to tug at my limbs.

"It does. But, we're in a time crunch, aren't we? The faster we either find evidence or eliminate him as a suspect, the better."

I grinned. Less than a week ago, I barely knew this man. Now, we were in this together. No matter how irritating I may have found Harrison Byrne, he was just my sort of person. He also had a point.

"All right. Give me a minute to dress." I turned to the wardrobe, the quilt pulled behind me to cover my backside.

"Shame you can't go in that. With your hair down, you look more like a goddess than usual."

I whirled around. "Harrison Byrne," I whispered with force, "Show some decorum."

He stifled a laugh with his hand. The fact the man was incorrigible did nothing to change what needed to be done. Maxwell Priest's home had to be searched, and time was of the essence.

In front of my wardrobe, I pulled a black dress from a hanger and moved behind the privacy screen. "You better stay put."

"I'm good with my hands if you need any help, Cora. Otherwise, I'll stay right where I am."

It would take me twice as long to button the dress on my own, but there was no way I would ever ask Harrison for help.

As I struggled into my gown the best I could, the clock in the hallway struck two a.m. A nervous energy gathered inside me. I'd never in my life been out this late. If Isabella caught me sneaking out, she would lock me in this room until I turned thirty. Of that, I had no doubt.

Dressed in my plain black gown, I slipped into my heavy wool coat. The night would be a cold one. I pinned my hair up the best I could, then wound a knit scarf around my ears. I tucked my gloves into my pocket, ready to meet the unusualness of the night head-on.

Rather than go back down the trellis, we tiptoed out my door and down the hallway. I paused long enough to notice there was no light issuing from beneath Isabella's door. The silence of the hall was oppressive. My nerves began to waver. The irrationality of what we were about to do hit me like a blow to the face. I paused at the top of the stairs. My courage waned as I gripped the banister.

Harrison, already halfway down the stairs, turned back to check on my progress. "What?" he mouthed.

I shook my head, flinging my hand out. Harrison took my meaning and ambled down the stairs. I crept after him. I had come this far, after all.

My heart resumed a normal rhythm once we were in the open air. As we moved away from my house, I peered up at every window. Not a light nor a shadow could be seen. Harrison had left Rex tied to a tree down the street. There was no buggy.

I pulled Harrison to a stop by grabbing his sleeve. "How are we supposed to get to Mr. Priest's?"

"You'll ride behind me. How did you think we would manage? I can't very well drive a noisy buggy down the road without attracting attention, and you can't get out Lady without waking Walters."

Of course, he would put me in this position. Harrison Byrne had me exactly where he wanted me: riding behind him, my arms clasped around him. He may have had me in a spot, but I would rather fall off Rex than hold Harrison around the waist.

Harrison mounted his horse then held his hand down to me. I groaned as I reached up. When I was settled, I leaned back as far as I could, my palms resting against Rex's backside for support. With my legs gripping his sides, I felt stable. The ride would be a tad awkward, but I would manage.

"Modesty aside, it would be more practical for you to hold on to me, Cora. You could easily lose your balance perched as you are," he said in front of me.

"My posture has nothing to do with modesty. I'm quite comfortable, thank you."

"Suit yourself." Harrison softly clucked his tongue. Rex began his walk down the road.

It was when Rex moved into a trot that I knew I was in trouble. Holding on the way I was, was impractical. I began to lean, dangerously, to the side. Even I knew when I was defeated. My hands shot around Harrison's waist, holding on for dear life. Underneath my grasp, I felt his stomach constrict. I was sure he was stifling a laugh, so I gave him a little pinch.

"Ouch," he said, the laughter dying in his throat.

As we rode, I thought about Mr. Priest and what led me to believe he was involved. There was just as much reason to think Mr. Hill, Wolf, or even Mother had something to do with all this. Mr. Hill and Wolf were both in need of money. And Mother, well, there was her involvement with Joe Williams.

Above all, Mr. Priest stood out to me. I didn't have any evidence to support my theory, only a quiver of doubt. It troubled me to think that I hadn't seen Wolf in some time. He kept busy with his various jobs about town, but did this also give him an opportunity?

Maxwell Priest lived close by. His house on Cascade was northeast of mine. Harrison pulled Rex to a stop behind a newly planted young oak tree in the back lot of the large home. I held Harrison's arm as I slid off the horse. The grass was wet, and I slipped a little as my feet hit the ground.

Priest lived on the corner. The windows of the house next door were as dark and deserted as those of Mr. Priest's. Harrison and I crept to the backdoor like the practiced sneak thieves we had become. He crouched down as he had at the boarding house, the same lock-picking set pulled from his coat pocket.

It was dark, hard to see. I stood back, allowing as much light from the half-moon and stars overhead to shine on the door as possible. Harrison seemed to work more by touch than sight. He fished the tools inside the doorknob, his ear close to the lock. Nothing happened. I felt a little tendril of fear beginning to wind its way around my belly. If he failed, this dangerous expedition would be for nothing. I would have to sneak back into my house, facing the possible wrath of Isabella with not a thing to show for my stupidity.

I heard a twang as Harrison pulled out the tools, repositioned, and tried again. My breath seemed louder to me than the ringing of church bells. I looked around, the nervous twinge in my stomach bordering on nausea. The night was still, and not a soul was about to save us.

As I gazed at the neighboring windows, I thought it was time to abort our mission. A click sounded as the lock released. Harrison let out an audible breath. He re-pocketed his tools, then stood, his knee cracking. It sounded like a shot in the night. He quickly opened the door and we were inside.

We stood in a back room, taking a moment to calm our loudly beating hearts.

"I thought for a minute that it wasn't going to work," he said, out of breath.

"Me, too. Let's get on with this. Where do we start?"

"We need light. Let's find some candles. I brought matches. Then we can split up to search more efficiently." He moved further into the pitch-black room.

A metal object, knocked over by his foot, rolled across the floor, clanging with each turn.

"Strike a match to see where you're going. We can't afford to break anything and give away that there was a break-in," I whispered. Logically, I knew we were alone. Still, it scared me to be too loud.

A flare of a match illuminated the space, giving off an acrid, sulfur smell. We were in a mudroom; boots and coats hung from hooks to the right. Off to the left were empty crates along with the empty metal milk can Harrison had kicked over.

We moved through to the kitchen. Harrison struck another match. He rummaged through drawers, the small light from the flame barely enough to see by.

He made a sound of exclamation. "Candles."

Harrison touched the match to a small taper candle, lighting the wick. He held this toward me, then pulled out another, lighting it for himself. "That's better," he muttered.

The thought of splitting up still didn't appeal to me, so I rationalized a plan. "Let's begin in his office together. That's the most likely place to hide Tesla's documents, anyway. If we don't find anything in there, we can split up and move to other areas of the house."

I had been in Mr. Priest's home before. The structure of the house was narrow and tall. A winding staircase took you up a full three stories. On the top floor was a little door, which led out to a small crow's nest. I had it on good authority that Mr. Priest enjoyed sitting out on his crow's nest with a pair of binoculars to spy on the neighbors.

Whether this was true or not, I hadn't any reason to dislike Mr. Priest. Even after the strange dinner of the other night, I felt no ill will toward the man. The last party I attended here with Isabella elicited only good memories. Mr. Priest's home had been en fete that evening. The night was warm, there was dancing and music outside, crystal glasses sparkled with champagne, and lively conversation bubbled from every corner. It was strange to think of Mr. Priest, or anyone I knew, for that matter, committing any sort of crime. I certainly couldn't imagine him capable of murder.

I led the way to the front of the house. The front corner room was Mr. Priest's office. Never had I been inside, the door was always closed to guests. What I had seen of the house on previous visits led me to believe Priest was a neat man, as it was always sparkling clean. His expensive furniture gleamed with fresh wax, and the Turkish rugs appeared as if they had never been walked on.

There was an unlived-in quality to the pretty home. It smelled brand new, like furniture newly freed from shipping crates. The large, darkly stained door of the office stood all the way open. I wasn't sure what I expected. I supposed since it was always off-limits, I thought the room may be a mess in relation to the rest of the house, papers overflowing from drawers, books stacked on every surface.

Everything was perfect. It didn't appear as if any actual work took place in here. The room was large, twice the size of the spacious living room. An enormous carved wood desk sat in the center, in front of a bay window that I knew looked over a small garden, the street beyond. The heavy, forest-green curtains were drawn against the night. Bookshelves lined the walls.

I perused one of the shelves, my candle held high. The books looked and smelled brand new. I imagined if I were to take one down and open it, the spine, unused to being opened, would crack.

"At first sight, this room looks like the office of a professor, but, really, it's a tomb," Harrison said behind me.

He was right. It didn't appear as if anyone ever used this room. I moved to where he stood near the desk, opening and closing drawers. I ran my hand over the black ink blotter. This, too, looked unused. There were four sharpened pencils lying in a perfect row to the right of the blotter, and a small globe sat on the corner to the left.

"No, it isn't a tomb, at all. This is how Mr. Priest likes to keep his things. I believe he may have the same eccentricities as Mr. Tesla, only different. If that makes sense. It must be difficult to have to keep everything so precise for the peace of one's mind." I was beginning to feel for Mr. Priest. This led to a pang in my conscience.

"Well, don't feel too bad for him just yet." Harrison was crouched over the bottommost drawer.

I moved my candle for a better look, but all I could see was the top of Harrison's head. "Why? Have you found something?"

Harrison stood with a piece of paper clutched in his hand. He set the paper on top of the ink blotter. "Only Tesla's drawing of his new telescope."

CHAPTER SIXTEEN

The candle nearly dropped from my hand. I reached out
to take the document from Harrison. "It can't be." I didn't
want to believe it, yet here was physical proof clutched in
my fingertips.

My hand shook as I surveyed the drawing. There was no
mistaking Tesla's barely decipherable scrawl written up,
down, and across the page. In the center was the object
itself; Tesla's never-before-seen telescope. Mr. Priest was a
thief. The thought was a disappointing one. I had known
Mr. Priest a long time, since I was a child. He was friends
with both of my parents, had been in our home and we in
his, many times. Images of him sneaking around, stealing
documents from Mr. Tesla assaulted my mind. I was
reminded of something Marsh once said to me: *We never
know anyone as well as we think we do.*

I thought of Priest as he sat in his crow's nest spying on
his neighbors. This was the behavior of a dishonest person.
Add to this his curious questions regarding Tesla and his
lab, and I supposed it made sense.

He must have hoped to benefit in some way from Tesla's
work; either monetarily or professionally. Possibly even
both. Perhaps he dreamed of Edison-level fame and had no

other way to get there except to take ideas that didn't belong to him.

"Where are the others?" Harrison asked as he rifled through drawers.

"He could have sold them already. Maybe he isn't as well off as he appears. Didn't you say that once about Sharp?" I peered at Harrison over the edge of the paper. "Priest recently purchased two new thoroughbreds. Maybe this is where the money came from."

Harrison stopped his search to look at me quizzically.

I handed him back the document. "This is a small town. There isn't much that escapes notice."

A drip of hot wax slid over the back of my hand. I winced, about to set the candle on the desk when Harrison stopped me with a gesture. "We can't leave any evidence of our snooping, Cora. Don't set that down. As clean as this man is, he'll notice a smear of wax immediately."

I grimaced as I looked down at the pool of wax gathering around the wick. If I didn't dump it out soon, it would be scalding its way down my flesh. "We have what we came for. Let's go." What more was there to talk about? I moved to leave the study, ready to make tracks out the door.

"Wait a minute," Harrison said. "If we take this out, we have to explain how it came to be in our possession. Are we going to tell people about our recent spate of criminal activity? My dad will kill me if he knows I have the lock-picking set. Not to mention what he'll do to me if he finds out the rest."

Harrison was right; we needed a better plan. A loud sigh escaped my lips. This became more and more complicated each day. I chewed on the inside of my cheek, gaze trained on the desk as my mind became clouded with too many thoughts. The document would need to be found by someone else, but how?

"We can tip off the police, hoping against hope they search the house."

"Right. Because why wouldn't they search the house of

the man who's threatened and bribed them?"

Another good point. My frustration mounted, as did the wax in my candle. "He can't possibly have them all in his pocket, but how do we know who to trust? What about ..." I trailed off, an idea forming on the periphery of my mind.

"Go on, Cora. I don't have a single idea."

"Someone has to find the diagram in front of witnesses. I have an idea, but I don't know how well it will work."

Harrison bobbed his head to get me to continue my train of thought.

"Dove is angry with me, boiling mad would be a good description. Perhaps I can entreat Mr. Priest to help me. He can invite Dove and Mr. Sharp over for dinner. We'll be here with a few other society people to make it look like a legitimate surprise party. Mr. Priest will tell Dove it was my idea as a sort of apology. I hate to use Dove for our purpose, but this will give me the opportunity to take care of two problems at once. We'll give my friend a lovely evening, then somehow find the paper at the end of the night. What do you think? Does it sound too crazy?"

Harrison chuckled. "It sounds downright diabolical, Cora. I think it will work. You'll have to let me know how it goes."

"What are you talking about? You're coming as my guest." Harrison and I had come this far together. There was no way I would do this without him.

His face lit up with a smile bright in the glow of the candle flame. I shook my head. Smiling back was involuntary. "All right let's get out of here. Put the diagram back exactly as you found it."

We left carefully, mindful of the orderliness of the house. Nothing must be left out of place. We didn't even snuff out our candles until we were on the back porch so as not to leave a smoky smell inside. The wax began to harden in the cold almost as soon as we were outside. We decided it was best to take the used candles with us. Hopefully, Mr. Priest wouldn't notice the absence of two small tapers. After witnessing the meticulousness of his house, I somehow doubted it and felt a little drop of nerves in my belly.

The air was as frosty as ever. I blew out my candle, my breath mixing with the smoke until it was impossible to distinguish which was which. My eyes were heavy from exhaustion, thoughts of my warm bed almost making me weep.

I waited for Harrison to lock the back door behind, again taking a careful look around. The windows of the neighboring house remained darkly still. I couldn't imagine what would happen if we were seen and didn't really want to think about it. The sky was clear tonight, black as midnight, but big, bright stars winked in the dark tapestry, along with the pretty moon. If my mind wasn't so troubled, the scene may have been an enjoyable one.

Even though the ride home was short, I had trouble keeping my eyes open for more than two consecutive minutes. My hands, clasped around Harrison, pinched one, then the other to keep myself alert. I didn't want to end up in a heap, wallowing in the mud.

The two of us continued to discuss my plan.

"Tomorrow morning, I'll get up early to go to the telegraph office. I'll send Mr. Priest a message to implore his help with the party. Once I receive a reply, I'll send out the invitations and make the rest of the plans. I hope to have this set up for no later than three days from now, the night after he returns."

"You're sure he'll agree?"

I considered this. Under normal circumstances, I would say unreservedly that he would. These circumstances were anything but normal. Mr. Priest was no longer a family friend, he was a criminal whom I didn't know at all.

"If he doesn't, we'll have to think of something else. I'm too tired now to contemplate other alternatives."

"What will we do in the meantime?" Harrison asked. He gave my hand a pat, then left his hand on top of mine.

Weary, I didn't bother to shake him off. His large hand

added an extra layer of warmth over mine. It was nice. I decided to ignore it. "Well, I'll have planning to do. We should let Tesla know where we are and that we hope to have a resolution in a few days' time."

"Why don't you invite him?" Harrison turned his head halfway when talking to me. Although I didn't think anyone would see or hear us, it was still best to keep our voices down.

"Invite him to the party? Do you think he'd come?" I wondered how Tesla behaved at social gatherings. It was hard to imagine him sitting, engaged in idle chit-chat with anyone.

"If you tell him what your plan is, and what is waiting in the bottom desk drawer of Priest's office, I'm sure he would love to."

"I agree. Tesla on the guest list may also add to the appeal for Mr. Priest. Tesla will have to understand that we are orchestrating the night, and he will need to act according to our directions, which may not be easy for him."

Harrison stopped Rex. I held on to his arm as I slipped off the side, onto the ground. Harrison tipped his pageboy hat. I jogged toward my house, knowing he would be watching me until I was out of sight. This made me feel another sort of warmth, the warmth of knowing someone was on my side.

Only an hour had elapsed since I snuck out of my house with Harrison. It felt like days as I slunk back up the staircase, my breath held in my throat. I had slipped out of my boots at the back door. They were clutched tightly by the laces in one hand as my other held up my skirts. The rustle from the crepe too loud for my liking.

I paused at the top of the hallway. All was quiet.

My room was like an oasis. Happy to make it, I closed the door behind me, a long breath let out in a sigh. My limbs were weary. As much as I wanted to, I couldn't drop my clothes on the floor. Mother or Marsh would see and wonder what I had been up to in the night.

I dragged my body to the wardrobe. I flung my boots inside then shrugged off my coat. All I wanted was to rip the gown from my body, but I forced myself to carefully unbutton the back.

Willow snored nearby, never having budged from the hearth. I hoped to soon be in dreamland myself.

My bed was a cloud floating in heaven. I was sure I would drop off to sleep the second my head hit the pillow. Instead, I continued to think. Would Mr. Priest allow me to use his home for a surprise party? Would Dove even accept the invitation? Would Harrison and I be able to orchestrate the evening, to culminate in the discovery of the diagram?

Everything depended on our success. Just as I drifted off, fear spiked deep in my heart. I sat bolt upright. For some reason, Harrison and I hadn't made the connection. Perhaps the idea was so horrendous, our minds hadn't allowed us the realization. If Maxwell Priest had the diagram, this meant he could also be our killer.

CHAPTER SEVENTEEN

The experimental station appeared deserted. The only telltale sign that Tesla was within was the open sliding metal door. He was rarely anywhere else. According to Harrison, he had taken to sleeping in the lab, going back to the hotel only to wash and eat. Eating seemed to be something he was doing less of, as he concentrated everything on his work.

The day would be a beautiful one; the skies were blue without a single cloud, the sun was bright, and the air was fresh, warmer than the day before. The sharp, metallic odors of the lab cut through the cleanness of the mountain air. I scrunched up my nose.

"Do you want to do the talking, Cora? It is your plan, after all."

Harrison and I sat in the front of his buggy. Rex drank from the trough in front of him, oblivious to the drama. I was ready to move forward with our plan, ready to see this through to the end.

Miraculously, I had slept the night before and now felt more invigorated than I had in days. After waking, I made out invitations to the party at Mr. Priest's, then dressed and slunk out of the house and into the buggy. I hadn't seen Isabella, nor did I wish to at present. There was a lot to contend with now: the murders of two men, Tesla's missing documents, Dove's and Isabella's anger toward me. *One thing at a time.*

The telegram had been sent off. Now all we could do was talk with Tesla and wait for Priest's response.

"I suppose so," I responded, not moving from my seat.

Harrison put his arm around me. I was happy to have it there, happy to have him touch me. I wasn't cold, but his hand was warm, comforting in a way I had never experienced before. My throat tightened. My heart was unsure, maybe even a little downcast. Dove and Mother were the two people who knew me the most. It hurt to make them angry, to feel like I couldn't go to them with the heaviness of what I was involved in. I had to make it right with them. I didn't know what I would do if they wouldn't forgive me.

Harrison gave my shoulder a squeeze. "What can I do, Cora? My guess is something else is going on beyond what we're dealing with."

I hadn't told Harrison about Isabella and Joseph Williams. It wasn't my secret to tell, so I would keep it to myself. My mother's affair had nothing to do with this case. Her presence in Joe William's life was merely a coincidence. I swallowed the hard knot that formed in my throat. "Nothing. I'm okay, just tired."

I moved out of his embrace to clamber down the side of the buggy. My graceless legs wobbled. The trepidation that rang within reverberated through my limbs.

"There you two are. Weren't we supposed to meet at the park this morning?" Wolf trotted toward us after disposing of a pile of rubbish by the trash heap.

Harrison hopped down next to me. I thumped my head with the palm of my hand. "I'm so sorry. We both forgot. It was a long night."

"The party wear you out?" Wolf stood in front of us. The sun at his back glowed like fire through his unkempt hair.

"Yes, but that isn't all. Harrison and I … we broke into Mr. Priest's home late last night."

Wolf stuck his hands on his hips as he rolled his eyes. "Cora, for the love—you are in over your head here. I would think you would want to protect her." Wolf's hard gaze shifted to Harrison, who held up his hands.

"I'm not qualified to tell her what to do. Cora makes her own decisions. Besides, I'm as interested in all this as she is."

Wolf shook his head, clearly disappointed with both of us. "Did you at least find something good?"

"You could say that. We found one of Tesla's missing documents," said Harrison.

Wolf crossed his arms in front of his chest. "Great. Now it's time to go to the police."

Harrison and I exchanged glances. I gazed back at Wolf. "Almost. We have a plan that should see all of this put to rights. Please don't say anything until we've finished this, Wolf. A couple more days and this will all be over."

"I hope you get the ending you're after, Bird. As for me, I'm out of it. I must think about my future with Anne Marie. I'm sorry."

I threw my arms around my old friend. "Don't apologize. We owe you for all you've done."

Wolf swept a quick kiss over the side of my hair and released me. "I'm off to help the Dansburys with a leaky roof. Be careful." Wolf inclined his head to Harrison and left us to our machinations.

We found Tesla in his wooden chair, ankle propped on his knee, notebook open in his lap. He gazed up at his oscillator. As we approached, I observed him. I couldn't imagine what sorts of thoughts this man must have from one moment to the next. He was a genius on such a grand scale that I wondered how many people in the world could truly understand him.

Tesla seemed lost in his mind. Harrison reached out a hand, waving it in front of Tesla's face as we stood next to him. Tesla started. I bumped Harrison with my elbow. "Rude," I whispered.

"Excuse me, sir. It wasn't my intention to startle you. You didn't hear us come in."

Tesla tossed his notebook on the ground, stretching his arms over his head. He yawned, something I'd never seen him do before. "That's all right. I was thinking about the strange signals from outer space again. One of the many problems I'm currently considering." He smiled at me, then Harrison. "What have my two detectives discovered? I'm hopeful you come to me with good news."

All eyes were now on me. This was my moment to tell Tesla all we had discovered and all that had happened in the last few days. Sweat threatened to gather under my arms and heat began to permeate my cheeks, yet I went on.

"It depends on what you consider good news, sir. I doubt this is it. There was another death. The police officer who wanted to meet with us was murdered—poisoned with what Dr. Miller believes was Spanish fly. It was … gruesome."

"Tell me you didn't witness this, Miss Croft." Tesla interrupted me, standing from his chair.

"I witnessed the aftermath, we both did, with Dr. Miller." I gestured to Harrison. I thought it best to skip over the party and the chaos of my personal life. "Harrison and I had begun to suspect Maxwell Priest."

At this, Tesla guffawed as he ran his hand over his chin. "This revelation doesn't surprise me in the least."

"I didn't think it would. Well, although not the smartest plan, we thought to search Mr. Priest's home for any evidence of his involvement."

"Wait one minute, Miss Croft. What do you mean— searched? Are you telling me you broke into Maxwell Priest's home?" Tesla's face was one of pure bewilderment.

I looked to the side, squirming in place in front of one

of the world's most famous men. "We did. I admit, it wasn't smart, like I said. But we had to know."

"And, did you find anything?"

"We did. We found the drawing for your new telescope. It was in the bottom drawer of Mr. Priest's desk. We left it there, for now, sir. Harrison and I have a plan."

I related to Tesla my idea for the party. To find the document in front of witnesses was paramount. There was no way the police could deny the statements of a room full of people, many of whom were prominent citizens of Colorado Springs, even if some of the officers were corrupt. Tesla listened with his full attention; his gaze never wavering from my face. When I finished, I watched him watching me, unsure of what his response would be.

Finally, he spoke. "I don't like this one bit, Miss Croft. I had no idea this would become so dangerous or so far-reaching. There are still so many questions, so many answers we don't have. How was Mr. Williams involved? Why kill him or the policeman you've mentioned? It seems a lot of bother for a few pieces of paper. I've never cared for Maxwell Priest, but I never thought him particularly ambitious."

"You never know what people are capable of, sir. Not really."

"That's true enough, I suppose." He took a little turn around his chair. "Sign me up, Miss Croft. I'll attend this little party. I got you both into this, and I will be there with you as we finish this affair. You've both put yourselves in enough danger."

It was hard to imagine that I would be in danger from a man I'd known all my life. Still, he could have murdered two people already.

"Since the two of you have to wait a bit for Priest's response, why not stay and help me? I believe I can get a higher voltage for the artificial lightning. Would you like to help me try? Consider it your reward for all the hard work outside of the lab."

My head snapped toward Harrison, the widest smile I'd had in ages plastered on my face. He grinned, too, made even more evident by his eyebrows shooting up toward his hairline.

Tesla gave us our instructions. Harrison tweaked the oscillator while I adjusted the coils. Tesla walked around as he checked and re-checked our work. The man was a perfectionist. Nothing was to be touched again until he gave his final approval. Tesla handed out darkened glasses.

"Very well, good job. Harrison, you and I will remove ourselves to that corner." Tesla pointed to a safe distance from the coils. "Miss Croft, you will throw the switch. There. Everyone will need to wear the glasses. Try your best not to look directly into the streams of light."

I regarded a large switch connected to a box with running wires that connected it to the coils and oscillator. Tesla handed me a large pair of rubber gloves. "I can do it, if you'd rather."

For a moment, I considered the gloves, uncertainty fluttering in my chest. Funny how a walk into a possible murderer's home hadn't frightened me nearly as much as it should have, but to throw a switch Tesla had triple-checked and thrown himself before caused a bit of nausea to roll through my stomach.

The gloves felt cool in my hand as I took them from Tesla, who now seemed to me a bit of a mad scientist. "No, sir. I want to do it."

"You'll be quite safe, Miss Croft. Never fear." He patted me on the back, then moved to the corner where Harrison waited with a glint in his eye.

I waited for Tesla to turn back toward me. The glasses went over my eyes. When Tesla inclined his head, I slipped on the too-big gloves. My hands gripped the switch's handle. I sucked in a big breath, holding it as I pulled the handle down. It was heavy, heavier than I expected. I had to fight with it a little, and my small biceps strained with the effort to bring it fully toward the ground.

The second the top of the handle pointed at the floor, the room lit up in the brightest light I had ever seen. Even through the darkened lenses, the light was blinding. The room crackled with such loud pops, I jumped several times over. The smell of a clean burn filled the room. I had never experienced anything like this. It was terrifying and beautiful.

"Now, Miss Croft," Tesla called over the din. I reached down to fight with the lever as I moved it back into the start position. As quickly as the lightning moved around us, it was gone.

The room was startlingly cold and silent in its absence. We all stood still for several minutes once the electrical show was over. Then, Tesla removed his glasses as he ran over to a large dial on the oscillator.

I was rooted to my spot, as Harrison must have been since he also didn't move. This was different than the lightning I had experienced from the anteroom. I thought the flash of light then had been bright, overwhelmingly loud. Standing in the same room, in such proximity to the strike, took the experience to a new level. My hair crackled, loose strands standing out from my head. My skin, too, tingled electrically. I knew I would never forget this moment as long as I lived.

"The biggest one yet." Tesla whirled to face us, suddenly seeming ten years younger. Never had I seen such a genuine, happy smile on his face. His eyes were alight with excitement. He pulled his notebook and pencil out of his back pocket, writing furiously on a fresh page.

He looked up long enough to regard me and Harrison, still in our respective corners. "You two may go. I have new calculations to make. Send my invitation round, and I'll be at the party." Tesla waved us away. I knew by now what he needed most was solitude. He and his mind worked best when they were alone.

I pulled off the gloves, depositing them on a stool with the glasses. My hands now smelled like rubber, and I wiped them on the side of my dress, as if that would help.

Harrison and I left the acrid smells of the lab for the crisp, fresh air outside. I took a deep breath, feeling a new appreciation for the work Tesla did.

"That was something, wasn't it, Cora?" Harrison walked a step behind me.

"Incredible," I breathed.

"Imagine what it's like to be him. No wonder the man never sleeps." The admiration was evident in Harrison's voice, but I felt it, too.

"Yes, he's truly one of a kind." I turned my face toward the warm sun, closing my eyes to soak up its heat. Though the day was still cool, the rays comforted my soul, as always.

I didn't want to leave. I wanted to stay, ask Tesla questions about the experiments. What was he ultimately hoping to achieve? What had he discovered since coming to Colorado? He didn't have the time to answer my queries. He had dismissed us, so he could work in peace. A teacher, he was not. He was a man with his own purpose.

With great reluctance, I climbed into the cart. On the way back to my house, a thought occurred to me. "You haven't been hiring out your buggy much lately, have you?"

Harrison shook his head with a laugh. "I've had a few other things going on. It's all right. I've a few bucks saved. Besides, this is a little more important. And, it's almost over."

It was almost over. The relief would be keen when Mr. Priest was in police custody, the rest of us going on with our lives.

"Thank you, Harrison, for all of your help. I don't know how I would've done all this without you." Even though I spoke to Harrison, it was hard to look him in the face. Instead, I stared off to the side, watching the scenery of people, horses, and buildings.

"I'm happy to help, Cora. I admit I didn't want to at first." He laughed. "How hard was it for you to say that?"

I bumped him with my shoulder, smiling, but still not

able to look at him. "Pretty hard."

We shared our first genuine laugh. I continued to lean against his hard shoulder.

Upon entering the front hall, I checked the silver tray for a message from Mr. Priest. Enough time had passed that I expected to have a telegram waiting for me. There was nothing. I even picked up the tray to peek underneath. My shoulders slumped with my disappointment. I hoped this didn't mean he would ignore me. Perhaps if I didn't receive an answer by the end of the day, I would send another message to let him know that Mr. Tesla was hoping to attend. This would tip the scales in my favor.

I walked farther into the foyer, looking around for any sign of Isabella. I wasn't ready to face her yet. How would we act in each other's company? Isabella must have felt some embarrassment. I know I did. She was right when she said she was a grown woman who owed me no explanation. She didn't. Still, a part of me couldn't help but think of my father with a pang. I had to tell myself that he would have wanted her to be happy, to continue to live her life.

I heard nothing but the usual sounds—the hall clock ticked away the seconds, cook and her assistant rattled pots and pans in the kitchen as they prepared the evening meal. My stomach growled at the thought. Not only had I not slept much, I hadn't eaten well either. Perhaps when this was over, the sick waves in my stomach would pass.

Sucking in a breath, I picked up my skirts and dashed for the stairs, taking two at a time, then continued down the hall to my room as if I were being pursued by some phantom spirit. I didn't stop until I was safe out of sight. Closing the door behind me without seeing or speaking to anyone felt like a small victory.

The room was warm; the soft scent of lavender from the dried sprigs on my mantle were pleasant and floral. I wondered if lavender spread around the experimental station would improve the smell. I smiled at the thought as I crossed to my bed. I doubted Mr. Tesla would like that.

I sat, unlacing one boot then the other. My feet ached. If I was being honest, my whole body ached with exhausting tension. I had the rest of the day to myself, so why not indulge in a steaming bath to soothe the anxiety away?

That was when I saw it; a folded telegram sat on my bedside table, along with another note. My gut lurched. I picked up the note and recognized Marsh's short script. *I didn't think your mother would want to see this.* Marsh knew more than she let on. She was correct, as always.

I tore open the top of the telegram, ready to devour its contents.

Happy to help, Maxwell Priest

The telegram was to the point. My spirits soared. We were nearly to the finish line. The bath would wait. It was time to send out the premade invitations and order the food and flowers. As much as I wanted to relax, there was too much to do, too much nervous energy to burn. This ordeal would be over soon. Dove would forgive me, Isabella would be proud of me, Mr. Tesla would retrieve his stolen property and remain to finish his work, and most important of all, Joseph Williams and Officer Daniel McAdams would have justice.

CHAPTER EIGHTEEN

Party preparations were in full swing. The invitations had all been sent. Our cook, Agatha, hired two former employees of the Antler's Hotel to help with food preparation and serving. Walters had been dispatched to have two cases of champagne sent to Mr. Priest's. The affair was to be a small, intimate reception, thrown by me to celebrate the joy of my best friend. Dove and Timothy Sharp would be kept in the dark as to the true nature of the evening, until the surprise could be revealed.

I had avoided Mother for more than twenty-four hours. With the party the following evening, I knew I had to break our silence and speak to her. After I finished the menu with Agatha, I went to Mother's study. She seemed to spend more and more time there. I imagined she wanted to avoid me as much as I did her.

A little part of me hoped she may be out, which would put off our awkward interview, through no fault of my own. A now-familiar surge of nausea swept through my stomach. As I rounded the corner of the hall, I squared my shoulders in preparation then stepped in through the open door of her private office. There sat Isabella bent over her books. It was ridiculous to feel this uncomfortable with my mother, who

A.D. BRAZEAU

had always been dear to me. Although not as close as Father and I had been, I never felt this level of awkwardness with Isabella.

I cleared my throat to alert her to my presence. "Good afternoon, Mother."

She turned her head in my direction. "Cora, I wasn't sure you lived here anymore."

The sarcastic comment was clearly understood. Best to ignore it. "Mother, I'm throwing a small, private party for Dove and Mr. Sharp tomorrow evening. Mr. Priest has been gracious enough to host the surprise. I hope you'll attend. Mr. and Mrs. Mackenzie will also be there."

Mother looked at me for the first time since we spoke of her relationship with Joe Williams. I feared I would feel strange to converse with her after such an acknowledgment, but I didn't. Instead, my heart was sad for her. My mother was a strong woman, the strongest I knew. Even a woman of her strength needed love and companionship.

A smile of genuine warmth spread across my face. If she worried at all about what she had told me, I wanted to put her mind at ease.

She returned my smile, her eyes glowing with warmth. We were past our awkwardness, it seemed. "Of course, Cora. I'm glad to see you've put your efforts toward something other than snooping. Dove needs you more than Mr. Tesla."

Mother had a way with words. She could make me feel terrible with the most succinct of sentences. She didn't chide me, only expressed an accurate statement. I wasn't sure when the change had occurred, maybe when she told me about Mr. Williams, but I began to understand her better. My mother was a woman who went her own way in the world, even when Father was alive, but she always did what she felt was her duty with her head held high. What she didn't need to know was the party would serve two functions.

"Yes, Mother. Dove does need me, and I plan to be a

170

less selfish friend. I needn't love her fiancé, only her."

I related the details of the party then left to finish preparations.

Nervousness evolved from a mild unpleasantness to a rolling sea of queasiness. The front porch of Maxwell Priest's home was as impeccable as I knew the interior to be. The perfect planks had been freshly scrubbed, the brass bell shone in the dying light from the sun, and the two matching rocking chairs sat side by side in a perfect row.

I stood in my emerald-green silk bustle gown with my black velvet wrap tight around my shoulders. Given the low temperatures of recent days, the evening was unseasonably warm. I should have been fine without my wrap. As it was, I shivered underneath the heavy velvet.

Harrison was next to me, his expression solemn, his figure sturdy and solid in my father's coat and tails. He was handsome, more handsome than I cared to admit. There was no glint in his eye or mischievous grin this evening. We were a pair on a mission. The discovery of Tesla's document would be my job, and mine alone. I would wander into the study, in search of a scrap of paper, and find the diagram. What came after, only time would tell.

Harrison rang the bell. As he did so, I pushed my arm through his, wrapping my fingers around his bicep. He pulled me in tighter, and although I avoided his gaze, I was sure the grin was there now.

Mr. Priest's butler opened the door and ushered us into the entryway. We were the first to arrive by design. I wanted to make sure all was in place. Not only did I mean to ensnare Priest this evening, I meant to win back my friend.

The house was warm. As we walked into the parlor, the fire crackled and popped, sparks flying against the screen. The flowers I had sent over were placed with perfection on the side tables and mantle, and the two large displays flanked the doorway. The hothouse flowers were vibrant, their perfume subtle.

Mr. Priest walked in, his coat and tails neatly pressed. "Good evening, dear Cora, how lovely you look. Green suits that dark hair of yours." He moved toward me, taking me gently by the shoulders, and pressed a light kiss on both cheeks.

"Mr. Priest, my friend Harrison Byrne." I stood back to indicate Harrison with a gesture. The two men shook hands.

"I must say, Cora, I was surprised to receive your request. It seemed strange to me you wouldn't rather host the evening in your own home."

"It wouldn't have been much of a surprise if I had, now would it?" I laughed, trying my best to affect a playful attitude.

Mr. Priest joined me, his own laugh more of a chortle. "I suppose not. Well, I'm happy to help. The evening should be a pleasant one. Will Tesla, himself, really be here?"

"He will. We will have to do our best to keep him entertained."

Before Mr. Priest could respond, the bell rang, again. I had purposely given the Mackenzies an invitation to arrive thirty minutes after everyone else. This would, I hoped, give the others time to arrive and get settled before Dove and Mr. Sharp strode through the door.

There would only be four other people in attendance besides myself, Mr. Priest, Harrison, Tesla, Mother, and the Mackenzies. Betty Rogers, formerly Worth, was a friend from school. She had married Frank Rogers, the local dentist, in a lovely summer wedding in the garden behind her parents' home, not far from me and Dove.

Gail and Melanie Sherbrook were also friends from school. They, too, lived down the street and used to win almost every childhood game we ever played. These ladies arrived at the same time as the Rogers and the chatter became deafening in an instant, in a way that made me smile. Mother was the next to arrive in a sapphire-blue silk gown that hugged every curve. She sat next to Mr. Priest, a glass of champagne gripped in one hand, while I played hostess.

It was lovely to catch up with our old friends while we waited for Dove and her entourage to arrive. These young women had all stopped going to school around the same time Dove did, about a year ago. I tried to enjoy the moment and concentrate on their stories, instead of thinking about seeing Dove and having Priest arrested. I was beginning to second-guess my plan when the bell rang again.

We were in this now, for better or worse. I took a deep breath, quieting down the guests the best I could. I knew Tesla would likely arrive last, so this must be Dove. We all stood, glasses of champagne bubbling in our hands as we faced the parlor entryway.

I heard the sing-song voice of my best friend in the hallway, as the bustle of the arrival and taking-off of wraps caused my stomach to dip into my toes. This was it. I had no idea how she would react to the sight of me. For all I knew at that moment, she could turn heel and walk out the door.

As luck would have it, Dove and Timothy were the first two through the doorway. Her face was full of astonishment with wide eyes as we all yelled, "Surprise!" in unison.

I moved forward, handing off my glass to Harrison while sucking in a deep breath. "Dove." I held my hands out to her. "I wanted to continue our celebration of your wedding in a more intimate setting and apologize for my behavior at Glen Eyrie." I said this last part mostly under my breath, not eager for the entire room to hear what I said, wondering what had taken place between us.

For a second, I stood in front of my friend, hands out awkwardly, while Dove stared. Then, slowly, by degrees, her face melted. She smiled all the way to her eyes as she grasped my hands in hers. "Oh, Cora, this is lovely." She pulled me to her, and we embraced as sisters, tears threatening to well up in my eyes.

I pulled away to stand back so Dove could meet the rest of the party. She shone like the sun in yellow silk, her blonde hair the crowning rays. Mother rose to greet Dove's parents, her old friends. For the first time, I looked at Timothy Sharp. I hadn't acknowledged him when he entered, but Dove didn't seem to notice. He now stood alongside her as she spoke with the three young women, we'd known all our lives. His attention, however, wasn't on their conversation, it was on me. His eyes were narrowed in what I would call a glare. Clearly, he hadn't forgiven me for Glen Eyrie, but I couldn't imagine why, unless he was being protective of his future wife.

Harrison moved next to me, thankfully diverting my attention away from the man who glowered near the fire. He pushed my glass back in my hand. "Drink up. It won't be long now."

This was a reminder that our mission was two-fold. I brought the glass to my lips, drinking deeply of the cool but sharp liquid. The bell rang for the final time. As it did so, I jumped, the champagne dribbling out of the glass and down my chin. I wiped it off with the back of my hand before it dripped onto my gown.

Tesla was ushered into the room, looking more dapper than I'd ever seen him. A diamond stickpin glinted in the lapel of his beautiful black jacket. His hair, usually slightly mussed, was oiled and slicked back with a precision that would make all other men jealous.

The room went deathly quiet. I had to look around to make sure there were still people in the house. Everyone stood at attention, except for my mother. She remained on the settee, a look of nonchalance on her face, as if she hadn't a care in the world. Mr. Priest had jumped to his feet and stood, a slight tremble in his hands.

Tesla regarded the room with a look I could not define. Although not quite as passive as Isabella's expression, he looked as if he would rather be anywhere else in the world than that parlor at that moment.

I took the situation in hand, trying to affect confidence when all I felt was unease. "Mr. Tesla, how wonderful of you to join us." I took him by the arm to steer him around the room.

Our first stop was our host, Maxwell Priest. "I believe you know Mr. Priest. He was generous enough to lend me his home for the evening."

The two men shook hands coolly, Priest barely able to look Tesla in the eye. This, to me, seemed like proof of his guilt. How often was the guilty child unable to hold the gaze of the reproachful parent?

Mother remained seated as I introduced Tesla. He reached down, pressing his lips gently to her fingertips. If I didn't know my mother better, I would have said she blushed ever so slightly.

After Tesla was introduced to the room, I left him in conversation with Dove and Mr. Sharp. The latter man continued to regard me with what I considered disdain. He barely seemed to pay Tesla any mind, by far the least interested in Mr. Tesla than anyone else in the room. If Tesla was still irritated by Sharp's intrusion in his lab, he didn't show it.

The champagne flowed. Finger foods were passed around as guests talked amiably with one another. I had secured Dove, and she and I sat on a divan, my back to her fiancé. I'd had enough of his scrutinization. The evening was wearing on. I knew I had to get to the desk soon. I wanted nothing more than to enjoy this night, to act as my old self without a care in the world.

Tesla sat with Harrison, Mother, and Maxwell Priest. Every now and then, I could feel his eyes on me, no doubt wondering when I would get on with it. There was no escape either way I turned.

Finally, I decided it was time to act. I patted Dove on the hand. "I'll be right back. Don't move." I winked. The steady stream of butterflies in my stomach took flight as I excused myself.

I slipped out the kitchen door. If Mr. Priest were watching me, he would think I wanted to check on things back there. I made a beeline straight past the bustle of Agatha and her helpers and stepped into the hallway. From there, I walked with unsteady steps to the office door. I was only just out of the line of sight from the parlor, so I moved fast, rolling the pocket door open only as far as I needed to step inside.

The room was exactly as we had left it. My heart thumped wildly in my chest. I pressed a hand to my breast to will the beating into a calm rhythm. I moved to the desk and pulled open the drawer a little too forcefully. It squeaked loudly. I thought my heart would stop. My gaze darted to the door and I froze for a good minute. No one came.

There, resting in the bottom of the drawer, was the document. I snatched it out, practically tripping over my feet as I ran to the door. I had to get this over with. I flew into the room faster than I meant to, the paper clutched in my hand. Every eye turned toward me; conversation halted.

I breathed heavily as I inhaled and exhaled in loud gasps. I focused on Tesla, who was watching me with a keen gaze. "I was looking for a piece of paper in order to write down a few words for a speech. I found this in Mr. Priest's drawer." I thrust the paper at Tesla, my hands shaking.

He snatched the paper as I shrank back from the room.

"This is an outrage," he shouted.

CHAPTER NINETEEN

Tesla was an incredible actor. Never did the performance feel fake, because the anger was real. After the confusion of the room died down, Maxwell Priest finally found his words.

"What is the meaning of this?" he demanded. "Cora, why were you snooping through my private things, and what is that?" Mr. Priest pointed at the paper still clutched in Tesla's hands.

Tesla waved the paper around. "This, sir, is a diagram, stolen from my lab. It is the third document to go missing since I came to this town. While this doesn't directly tie you to the murders, it certainly ties you to the theft. The police can work out the rest."

Mr. Priest's eyes bulged out as he stared. "Murders," he sputtered. "What murders?"

I balled up my fists in my dress in an effort to keep my composure. I stepped forward to speak for the first time since handing off the document. "The murders of Joseph Williams and Daniel McAdams. Mr. Williams was likely your accomplice, while Mr. McAdams was bribed to keep quiet. Only he decided he couldn't keep quiet any longer, so you poisoned him."

There were loud gasps of shock around the room. I noticed Mother flinched at the name of her friend Joe Williams. There would be hell to pay with her later.

To my surprise, Timothy Sharp moved next to me. The man who had glared at me all night took charge. "Mr. Mackenzie will go and collect the police. I'll stand right here and make sure this criminal doesn't move."

The look on Mr. Priest's face was one of pure shock. Shock at being found out. His cheeks were bright red as he continued to mutter nonsense to himself. Beads of sweat formed at his hairline. I pulled my attention from him long enough to gaze at everyone else in the room. Dove remained seated as I had left her, poised confusion wrinkling her brow. The other ladies—Mrs. Mackenzie, Betty, Gail, and—Melanie stood huddled together near the mantle. The gentlemen, including Harrison, moved in a protective ring around the room, I assumed to keep Mr. Priest from fleeing.

Lastly, my gaze fell on my mother. I thought she would be shocked, sad even, at the pronouncements of the evening, but her cool eyes were on me. Her mouth formed a smirk that spoke of disappointment. Did she know what we were about? I wouldn't have been surprised if she had.

Avoiding her eyes, I looked at the floor, then back at our possible murderer. Mr. Priest seemed to have recovered himself. He took out his handkerchief, wiped his brow, and held up his head.

"May I look at the paper in question, Mr. Tesla?"

"There's no use in denying it, Priest. We've caught you red-handed. Here." Tesla shoved the paper into Priest's hand.

Mr. Priest held up the diagram, scrutinizing the page, even turning it over. "I've never seen this in my life." The paper was thrust back toward Tesla. "The outrage, ladies and gentlemen, is that I've been accused of abominable crimes. I've never stolen a thing from Mr. Tesla. I've never harmed a hair on anyone's head. To believe this nonsense, is just that, nonsense. As I'm a rational man, I will sit and wait for the police. They will sort all this out."

Mr. Priest did sit, and he did wait. None of us moved for the next twenty minutes. When the police showed up at the door, Mr. Mackenzie tagging along, they removed Mr. Priest to the dining room and put a guard on him. Captain King, his presence large and bulky, then took us all, one by one, into Mr. Priest's study to question us individually about the events of the evening.

When it was my turn, I related all that had occurred over the last several days, beginning with the body of Joseph Williams. I even told the captain about our search of Mr. Williams's room, and how I snuck around Officer McAdams's home. The only element I omitted was how we found the paper in Priest's desk during our second breaking and entering. Harrison and Tesla would also leave this bit out.

"Well, Miss Croft, that's quite the story. Hard to believe such a thing has happened in our town. You, young lady, have put yourself in situations you shouldn't have. You're lucky you didn't get hurt or in trouble. I should arrest you and your friend, along with Mr. Priest."

A pit formed in my stomach. I hadn't thought that we too could get in trouble. We had, after all, unmasked a killer. Surely, that was good for something.

Before I could form an excuse or apology, the captain continued. "As it is, I don't see that any harm was done. But, for now on, please leave police business to the police."

The tension in my body eased. I wanted nothing more to do with dead bodies or stolen property. "I'll be happy to, Captain. I only wanted justice for the deceased gentlemen, and for Mr. Tesla to retrieve his work."

Captain King nodded. "I assured Mr. Tesla a thorough search of the premises will be conducted. For now, you may all leave."

Harrison was the last to be questioned. I waited outside for him with Tesla. The others had long gone, Isabella, too.

She hadn't waited for me. I was slightly stung, but if she had, I wouldn't be able to debrief the evening with my accomplices.

I shivered in my wrap as Tesla appeared unbothered by the falling temperature. There was a familiar smell of snow in the air. I hoped Harrison would be out in time to get us both home before the flakes began to fall.

"This whole affair has been highly distasteful, Miss Croft. I'm glad to see it at an end. Now, I can finally get on with my work." The diagram for his telescope was folded neatly, grasped in one hand. "I only hope they can retrieve my other documents."

"I'm sure they will, sir. It can only be a matter of time before all your property is returned to you." I paused, looking up at the star-filled night. "I'm so glad you'll stay to finish your plans. I'm so looking forward to getting back to a normal schedule."

Tesla chuckled. "I'm not sure what a normal schedule is. I've never kept one of those. In fact, I'll be up most of the night as I prepare for tomorrow."

"Tomorrow?" I inquired.

Tesla looked toward me out of the corner of his eye. "Tomorrow, I will be working on my electrical signals. I expect you to be at the experimental station no later than nine a.m."

I bit my bottom lip to keep my excitement from seeming too evident. Despite my best efforts, a broad smile broke out across my face. "I'll be there, sir."

Harrison joined us not long after, his own smile firmly in place. Tesla shook our hands, congratulating us on a job well done, before he left us alone in the night.

"We should write a book about our adventures, Cora. We'll call it *Young Detectives*, or something like that," Harrison said on the way home.

I patted his hand. While I did so, Harrison took the opportunity to grasp my fingers, giving my hand a warm squeeze. I held him back, unable to pull away this time.

Instead of a blush or an embarrassed look off to the side, I kept my face turned toward his as he drove. "I'll leave the writing up to you," I teased.

We drove home, hand in hand on the driver's seat of the buggy. I was relieved for the drama to have ceased but would miss my late-night adventures with Harrison.

Rather than spring down from the buggy as I was wont to do, I allowed Harrison to get down first then clasp my waist as I descended. We stood for an awkward moment, face to face, alongside Rex, who disturbed the silence with chomps at his bit.

I laughed. Then I did something that took us both by surprise. I stretched up on my tiptoes and kissed Harrison Byrne on the mouth. The movement was quick, the kiss not lingering, but it was enough to ignite something within me I hadn't known was there.

Harrison's smug smile was gone, replaced by a look of true astonishment. He stood in front of me, hands still firmly around my waist, silent as the grave.

"Lost your tongue, Harrison Byrne? Well, goodnight then." I reached up for another kiss, this one a little longer than the first, then turned toward the house, stepping out of his embrace. I pressed my hand to my mouth, stifling a giggle as I imagined Harrison watching after me, his mouth agape.

I expected to find Isabella in each room I moved through. The hall was silent and black. Not a single lantern had been left lit to wait for my arrival. The dining room was also deserted. I bounded up the dark stairs, candles to light my way unnecessary. I thought perhaps I had escaped her disdain when I opened my bedroom door and a dark figure moved near the window. She had watched me kiss Harrison. My stomach tightened with the expectation of the barrage to come.

"Mother, you should be in bed," I began.

It was then I froze. The figure at the window was not my mother. No one else would stand in the dark so. My hand still gripped the doorknob. I felt a scream well up in the back of my throat. Moments away from slamming the door open, the figure moved into the light.

"Dove," I breathed out a sigh of relief. "What in the world? You scared the life out of me. Why didn't you light some candles?"

I moved into the room, my gloves and bag thrown on the chair. I could make out everything inside only from the light of the moon as it streamed through the window. I struck a match to light two candles on the dresser. A warm glow filled the space. I was tired, weary to my bones. All I wanted was to sleep, enjoy the victory of the evening.

"Something nags at the back of my mind. Mr. Priest didn't confess as I thought he would. He doesn't seem the type of man capable of hiding such secrets." I ignored Dove for a moment and sat at my writing desk. Inside was the slip of paper that held the name of my one suspect. I pulled it out and spread it on top of the mahogany surface.

Maxwell Priest. "No, this is wrong."

Next to come out was the hanky-wrapped cigarette and the swath of silk. It was then I remembered what awaited at the bottom of the handbag I carried the night of the party at Glen Eyrie. How stupid of me to forget. I bolted to the top drawer of my bureau. There sat the beaded bag. I unsnapped the clasp and reached inside. The night of the engagement had been such a disaster. I'd felt so ill, I'd fought with Dove, found out about Mother and Joe Williams, then snuck out for a middle-of-the-night break-in with Harrison. No wonder I'd forgotten, but still, such an important detail should have been examined.

"Ogden Gold," I whispered. Harrison did say this was a brand smoked by gentlemen. My stomach sank to my toes. A coincidence, surely. Maxwell Priest had the document in his desk drawer. He was our killer—he had to be.

I realized Dove hadn't spoken or moved. "Dear, whatever are you doing here?" I turned toward her. The shock of my friend's face nearly sent me backward into the dresser.

For a moment, I thought the red mark on Dove's cheek must be from the light of the candle. She stood in front of me like a still apparition. I wasn't even sure she breathed.

"Dove, what's going on?" I moved toward her, seizing her by the shoulders. She winced and I released her. "Why is your cheek red? You look as if you've been struck. Dove, talk to me. Did someone hit you?"

Tears spilled from her eyes. She let them fall without wiping them away. "Cora, I'm so sorry," she whispered.

CHAPTER TWENTY

"Sorry for what? Dove, you're scaring me. Tell me what's happened."

"I can't. He'll kill me." Her body began to shake violently. Instead of moving to help herself, Dove continued to stand in front of me like a ghost.

I pulled a quilt from my bed and wrapped it around her shoulders. Steering her toward the bed, I pushed her gently until she sat on the edge. Her words had spiked a thrill of terror in my heart. I wanted to slap her, to pull her out of whatever trance she was in. To discover the meaning behind what she was saying was paramount. I did my best to keep my cool.

"Dove," I said, gently. "Who will kill you? Mr. Priest?" Sitting next to her, I moved my arm around her shoulders. Still, she was silent as she stared out into space.

"Did Mr. Priest threaten you, dear? He's going to jail. There's nothing more to fear from him." I huffed a sigh, my head began to swim. Did we have it all wrong, after all? "I'm sorry if the evening was frightening for you." I wondered if the revelation at Priest's home had traumatized her somehow. The trancelike fear she was in could be interpreted as such, but it did nothing to explain the bright red streak across her face. "Or was it someone else? Mr. Sharp, perhaps?"

We were getting nowhere, and my patience wore thin. I was tired. The sooner Dove snapped out of it, the better for both of us. I tightened my grip on her shoulder and gave her one good shake. "Dove, look at me and tell me what's going on," I said, sharply.

Her head whipped around, her eyes wide as if she'd just seen a horrible sight. "I have to go. I shouldn't have come. This was a mistake; it's all been a mistake." Dove jumped to her feet, the quilt falling to the floor, and flew out the door.

I didn't know what to do. I couldn't let her walk home alone in the dark, so I followed, at least so far as to make sure she was safe. Surely, she was spewing nonsense. My friend had never seemed so frail to me as she did now. The more I thought back on the evening, I couldn't see how she should have been bothered so. Something else was going on.

The hallway was quiet, which surprised me. I thought after the commotion, Isabella would bound out of her room to see what the matter was. For a mad second, I thought to wake her. The folly of sneaking around in the dark suddenly hit me. The captain was right, I had put myself in danger; we all had. As soon as I saw Dove home, I would lock my door tight, and there would be no more skulking about.

I picked up my skirts and dashed down the stairs. The back door was left wide open. This was the way Dove had made her escape. The girl was clearly not in her right mind. I stepped out in the night, a chill spiking its way down my spine. I didn't like the dark. I certainly didn't like being alone in the dark in the middle of the night. Dove was nowhere to be seen. I would have to walk out farther in order to see her. I moved toward the south side of the house, toward the Mackenzies'. Dove didn't have much of a head start on me, so I should have at least seen her in the moonlight, running across the lawn. There was no one.

Perplexed, I looked around. A dark figure moved out

from behind the bushes so fast, I couldn't register what happened. One moment, I was trying to find Dove, the next, a sharp pain obliterated all sense.

Blinding light throbbed behind my eyelids. The pain in my head was intense, mind-numbing. Although the grass was cold, it was soft, comforting. For one mad moment, I wanted to keep my eyes closed and sleep. Then I remembered why I had been out in the first place.

My eyelids flew open. The dark sky twinkled with bright stars overhead. Flat on the ground, I looked around. There seemed to be no one about. All was quiet. Rolling over to my side, I tentatively pushed myself into a sitting position as pain sliced through my head. What had happened? I pressed my hand to my temple then pushed my fingers farther back, exploring my scalp.

"Ah," I cried involuntarily as I probed what felt like a gash in the back of my head. I tried to think. Dove had vanished. There was a figure. The figure had rushed me in the dark with such speed, I couldn't see who it was. That person must have hit me over the head and left me, unconscious, in the grass. But who?

It couldn't have been Dove. She would never strike me, nor would she have any cause. Besides, Dove always wore the same floral perfume. The scent of the French cologne lingered in my room as Dove stood by the window. Had I not been convinced it was Isabella who watched me from behind the curtains, I would have recognized it.

There had been someone else out here, someone who watched from the shadows. I wobbled to my feet, my gaze on the ground to help me keep my balance. I blinked back tears to clear my eyes of the fog clouding my brain.

What to do now was the question. Did I run back inside, bar the door, and cower under my covers? As mad as it seemed, there would be no cowering. I needed to know what was going on. If Dove could sneak into my home, I could sneak into hers. Being long-standing friends, each home contained a key for the other to use in emergencies and such. The key to the Mackenzies' house hung from a hook in the kitchen.

I darted inside the still-open door, careful to take a look around. For a moment, I worried whoever had hit me had made their way inside my house. I could detect no movement, nor could I hear any sound other than the tick of the clock. Something seemed to click into place in my mind. The person who attacked me wasn't interested in the occupants of this house, they were watching Dove. I should get help, wake Isabella, run for Walters in the carriage house, but doing so would take time I didn't have. I needed to act, and to act *now*. Dove was the one in danger.

I hurried to the kitchen through the pocket door and tore the key off the hook with such force that the hook fell from the wall onto the tile floor with a clang. Without stopping to think through my actions, I sped off, back out of the house, across the expanse of lawn that separated our homes.

The grass was slick with dew. I tried to be careful but found my feet slipping more than once in my haste. My only thoughts were of Dove. I feared the phantom had gone for her after attacking me.

Out of breath, I bounded up the back steps to the door. Dove's house was similar to mine, except for the color. While ours was all whites and grays, Dove's was a colorful mix of blues in three different shades. The back door was painted a baby blue, the color of the sky at midafternoon.

I pushed the key into the lock as my heart threatened to beat its way out of my chest. Practiced as I was at entering a home without permission, this time the circumstance was different. Not only was the home occupied, I feared my friend was in mortal peril.

The key turned effortlessly in the well-oiled lock. I entered into the kitchen. The room was cold, lifeless, the fire from the stove long out. A thought occurred to me.

With the door securely locked, perhaps Dove was safe and sound in bed, after all. Would an attacker lock a door behind themselves? Maybe this was all my imagination. It was possible there hadn't been a figure, and perhaps a deer or a stray dog had knocked me down and I'd hit my head. With all the craziness of these past days, it could have been simply my exhausted mind playing tricks on me. My brain was muddled.

I almost decided to go back home, but since I was here, and had already entered the house, I may as well check on Dove. I crept through the kitchen and made my way down the long hallway to the front stairs. I could have taken the servants' stairs from the back of the house, but they were small and uncarpeted. There was less chance I would be heard if I took the large, winding staircase that began not far from the front door.

I moved up the stairs, one at a time. After every other step, I stopped to listen. The Mackenzie house was as quiet and dark as my own at this time of night. Dove's room was in the southwest corner of the second floor. She had a spectacular view of the mountains I was always jealous of.

Her door was ajar. I paused at the threshold. There was no light or sound within. Unsteadily, I reached out a hand, pushing the door inward. I remained where I was, peering into the room the best I could in the dark. The curtains must have been pulled tight. It was impossible to see anything beyond where I stood.

I took a step inside, again with a pause to look around. My heart, which should have calmed down by now, hammered away in my chest. I did my best to level my breathing but was afraid my heavy breaths were quite loud, certainly audible to anyone who may be in the room. My nerves were frayed beyond repair. I shook my head. I was being irrational. I had nothing to fear in a room where I had spent so many days and nights playing games, braiding hair, and talking about the future.

Stop seeing conspiracies that aren't there. With that, I

proceeded with confidence toward the bed. I may not have been able to see in the dark, but I knew exactly where I was going. When I reached the edge, I peered down, running my hand over the satin coverlet. Empty.

My heart began to race in earnest. I moved back to the door, closing it with a soft whoosh. I became an automaton, operating with determination. My next stop was Dove's bureau. In the top drawer, she kept a book of matches. I pulled these out and struck one, the sulfur a bright flash burning in the dark. The flame was touched to the wick of two candles atop the mantle. The room lit up. My eyes took a moment to adjust.

The space was empty of human occupants. Where on earth was Dove? Fresh fear spiked through my body in sharp waves. I moved frantically about the room as I tried to decide what to do next. Her parents must be woken, the police alerted. I had gone as far as I could on my own. If she wasn't here, she must be in danger.

My gaze fell on a jewelry box by her bed. The box sat on the nightstand. It was brand new, or new to me, as I had never seen it before. The container was a dark mahogany inlaid with swirls of mother of pearl along the edges. This must be a gift from her fiancé to house her new gifts. Something about the contraption called me to it.

I attempted to lift the lid. It was firmly locked. Pulling a hairpin from my bun, I bent and twisted it until it resembled a pick from Harrison's bundle. This I stuck into the lock, moving it every which way until I heard a click and felt the top of the box release.

The lid fell back to reveal what I expected to see. The opulent diamonds Dove had worn at the party at Glen Eyrie were nestled on the top over a carpet of black velvet. I picked up the necklace. As I did so, the bottom of the box moved. I set the necklace on the table, then the earrings. With one finger, I pressed on one side of the velvet. The opposite end popped up. This I pulled back. Underneath was another compartment. It seemed all the women in my life kept secrets.

There were several letters and a silver tin. The letters were pulled out one by one. They were all addressed to Dove from her fiancé, Timothy Sharp. This was not surprising. Suitors sent their lovers letters all the time. My guess was these notes were filled with the gushing of sweethearts. I set these aside and picked up the tin. I expected to find another piece of jewelry inside. My thumb pushed the small, hinged lid until it popped off and flew back.

The contents inside took my breath away. It was like I knew as soon as the odor wafted out. I almost dropped it on the floor but steadied myself before it fell from my fingers.

I felt ill. My vision blurred. I caught myself against the side of the bed with one hand, the tin gripped tight in the other. The coarse powder was odd, but there seemed nothing else it could be. I closed the tin to take a closer look at the lid. *Spanish flies.* But, why would she have Spanish flies? She couldn't be the murderer. What would Dove possibly have to gain from the deaths of two men and stolen documents from Nikola Tesla? It didn't make sense. Exhaustion clouded my mind as I tried to think on the last several days, on all the revelations and people involved.

The torn glove. Dove's glove was torn the day she told me of her engagement. But the hole was small, and it was before Officer McAdams was poisoned. Did it fit in the timeline? It was hard to think straight. She had been in the lab the day the diagram went missing. Perhaps the hole in the glove was a sign she needed money. It was possible the Mackenzies were not as well off as they once were, which would also explain her haste to marry Sharp. Dove had said, *He'll kill me.* Suddenly, I felt unsafe in this home. Had her father put her up to this? With the pounding in my head, I couldn't think straight.

She couldn't have done this on her own, but who was her accomplice? Priest? Sharp? Her father, of all people?

The matching cigarettes damned Sharp, that was true.

I had to think of what to do. Perhaps she wasn't in danger, after all. Perhaps, in her guilt, she had knocked me out and fled. If I alerted the police, they would track her down, arrest her. She would hang for her crimes. If I didn't, an innocent man would hang instead. Maxwell Priest must be innocent. I must speak with someone further removed from these people. Someone with the most rational mind of anyone else I knew. Before I sounded the alarm, I would talk with Tesla. He would know what to do.

CHAPTER TWENTY-ONE

The carriage house was dark, the scent of the sleeping horses musty and earthy. Although I tried to be quiet, I didn't much care if I woke Walters. I had to get to the experimental station as quickly as possible.

Never had I moved my saddle with so little trouble. Nervous fear was giving me strength I didn't know I possessed. Poor Lady was fast asleep on her feet.

"I'm sorry, girl. I promise lots of sugar cubes when this is over," I whispered to my drowsy horse.

Lady neighed loudly. Walters stirred overhead, as I feared he would. He would be down soon to check on the commotion. I continued working the saddle into place, determined to ride out of here with as little trouble as possible.

"Miss Cora, is that you?" Walters hobbled down the wooden steps, a candlestick held aloft in his hand.

"Yes. I'm sorry to have woken you, Walters. There's been an emergency, and I have to get to the lab."

"What's happened?" His voice was murky with sleep.

"I can't say. Not until I know all the details. Please don't worry—I won't be long." This was a lie. I was sure I wouldn't be back anytime soon.

I mounted Lady in my silk gown and wrap, riding out into the night. It was dark, but the moon and stars provided enough light to allow me to make out the road and any large obstacles. These streets were as familiar to me as my own face. Making my way through town wasn't the hard part. The hard part was what came next.

Halfway to my destination, I wondered if I should check Tesla's hotel, before riding all the way to the lab. Something told me, with all the interruptions he'd faced, he would want to get in as much work as possible. It wasn't unusual for him to fall asleep there. The experimental station was where I was sure to find Mr. Tesla.

I paid little mind to the frostiness of the night. I only wanted to get to the lab. Tesla would know what to do. My hands gripped and fidgeted with the pommel of my saddle as I worried over my friend, terrified to think about what could happen to her. She would be arrested … or worse. I thought back to the day she snuck into the lab. Her excuse had been one of curiosity. Now, I saw her visit as much more sinister. That was the day the last document was stolen.

I coaxed Lady into a faster trot. We needed to hurry.

The dark outline of the lab loomed ahead. I was still far off and couldn't make out any lights in or around the building. My heart sank as I thought about all the time wasted to ride out to the field. I almost turned Lady around to head back for Tesla's hotel when the wink of a dim light within sparked in the darkness.

He was there. No doubt he fell asleep and was now re-awakening to his work. For the first time, I was truly grateful for his strange work habits. This burden I carried would soon be handed off, placed in the capable hands of a man I barely knew but trusted implicitly.

I walked Lady up to the trough, jumped down, and tied her to the pole. I was too excited to walk, so I broke out into an all-out run for the front door. Unsurprisingly, it was ajar. Tesla couldn't be bothered with such things as closing it to the outside cold.

I pushed it the rest of the way open, stumbling in. Something tripped me. There was always a stack of empty crates next to the door. It appeared one had fallen over, several boards breaking off in front of the threshold. I shook my head. Something else Tesla couldn't be bothered with.

A lamp was lit, sitting on a chair near the oscillator. The chair was the very one Tesla used when sitting and thinking over his notebook, his ankle resting on his knee. The man himself was nowhere to be seen. I moved toward the chair, checking all around me as I walked. The place seemed deserted.

"Mr. Tesla," I called out softly. I stopped, waiting for a response I was sure would come. When none came, the hairs on the back of my neck stood up. I turned in place, straining to see all corners of the room. Maybe he fell back asleep in the anteroom.

As I walked toward the open door leading into the back room, I caught a glimpse of a garment. That one bit of silk caused my blood to run cold. I froze.

"Dove!" I shouted, willing myself forward.

I darted for the anteroom, catching myself on the doorframe to stop my forward motion. Dove was there, lying unconscious on the floor. The space was small. With her feet toward me, I had to skirt around her to reach her head. I dropped to my knees, placing a hand to her cheek.

"Dove," I said, again. Her cheeks were ice-cold, but she was breathing. Her breath, shallow and slow, alarmed me. "What is going on?" I asked my unconscious friend.

The sound of a step behind me sent my heart into my throat. "Dove lost her nerve, Miss Croft. That's what's going on."

I jerked around so fast I fell backward on my behind. A sharp pain jolted through me. The man at the door was Timothy Sharp.

"What have you done to Dove? And where is Mr.

Tesla?"

"Dove will be fine—for the moment. You two just wait here."

Before I could respond, Sharp slammed the door shut. Metal scraped against the floor, and something thumped against the door. He had pushed the shelving to block it. I scrambled to my feet. Using my shoulders, I tried to push the door open with all my might. It wouldn't budge. My body was so tired, my head so confused, I sank down to the ground. I refused to give up, refused to cry. I crawled back to Dove. She would have to wake if we were going to get out of here.

"Dove, I'm sorry, but wake up." I took hold of her shoulders and shook her, hard. Her head lolled to the side, but she moaned.

"Come on, Dove. I need you." I shook her again.

Dove's eyelids fluttered open about halfway. "Cora," she said, her voice a whisper.

"Yes, we're in trouble. You need to wake up."

She laughed, closing her eyes as she did so. Either she was out of her mind or she was giving up.

"This doesn't seem very funny to me. Open your eyes and tell me what's going on. Though, I think I can guess."

"What's going on is I've ruined my life, and many others in the process. All for a man I thought I loved."

"It was Timothy Sharp all along. And you helped him. But why?" The disappointment in my voice was obvious.

Dove rolled over, away from me. She sat up, then wrapped her hands around her skull. "Oh, Cora. You wouldn't understand."

"Try me. At the very least, you owe me the truth."

"I thought he loved me, Cora. It was only supposed to be one piece of paper, that was all. He made it sound so innocent. Just slip the paper in your purse, Tesla will never miss it."

"Why? Why did Timothy Sharp want Tesla's papers?"

"To sell them. There are scientists all over who would

give any amount of money for anything from Tesla."

"But Timothy Sharp doesn't need money that badly. Those diamonds he gave you alone must be worth a fortune."

"I'm not sure if he came by those diamonds through legitimate means. He does need money. His railroad scheme fell through, and he's up to his ears in debt. I didn't want to do it, Cora. Really, I didn't. He convinced me it was a one-time situation, and I caved."

"Joseph Williams and Daniel McAdams?" I couldn't think for a moment that Dove had killed those men.

"Timothy killed Joseph Williams. I had no idea, not at first. Timothy confessed later, after he tried to convince me to put the Spanish fly in Officer McAdams's food. He said he'd already had to kill one man; he didn't think he should have to kill another. He said if I poisoned the food, it would just scare the man, and he would stop making trouble. But, it did more than scare him. He died, Cora, by my hand."

My head was beginning to throb with all the information Dove was throwing at me. "Let's start with Joe. Why did he kill him?"

"Joe provided a couple of documents for Timothy for a fee. Joe started to feel that he'd done something wrong and told Timothy he was going to confess to Tesla. Timothy flew into a rage and pushed him out the window. I swear, I didn't know about it, Cora. Not until later. By then, I was in too deep. Timothy bribed the officer to make sure the death was written off as an accident. Then, he, too, grew a conscience. Timothy gave me the box of Spanish flies. He told me to put the powder in his food. He said they would just make him sick, as a threat. I had no idea what would happen, Cora. You have to believe me." At this, Dove broke down. She threw herself into my arms, her face pressed into my neck. Tears spilled out of her eyes, sliding down my chest.

I didn't know what to feel. Dove was in this. She was in this as deeply as Timothy Sharp. That she felt true remorse,

I had no doubt. Remorse would do nothing to repair the damage done.

"And Mr. Priest? How did the document get there?"

Dove trembled in my arms. "You made him nervous. Timothy left the engagement party early, right after you. He said he had an idea to buy us time. Later, he told me what he'd done and that he would call in a tip to the police when Priest returned from San Francisco. You beat him to it. I knew Mr. Priest would hang, but I was so afraid of Timothy by then, I didn't do anything." A loud sob escaped Dove as she cried into my neck.

I put my arms around her. Despite it all, she was my friend. "The first thing we have to do is get out of here. The rest we can sort out later. What do you think he means to do to us?" I already knew the answer. "Never mind. Don't answer that." We were in a world of trouble.

Dove pulled herself together. The two of us stood, ready to attempt to force the door. I hoped both of us working together could push the shelf far enough out of the way to allow us to escape one by one.

I gripped the handle, and side by side, we pushed, leaning in with our shoulders, shoving with everything we had. Little by little, the shelf began to give way. We huffed until there was just enough space for one body.

I slipped out first. Dove, holding my hand, was right behind me. We moved silently, gliding into the large room like wraiths. Timothy Sharp wasn't there. I gave Dove's hand a tug and we flew toward the door. We didn't make it far.

There was a scrape of dragging feet, and Sharp was walking through the doorway, a metal can in one hand.

He saw us immediately. His face changed, working itself into a sinister smile that made my blood run cold. "I hope the two of you don't think you're going anywhere." He dropped the can, liquid sloshing from the top. It was kerosene. The sharp smell of it assaulted my airways. He meant to burn the place down with us inside.

Sharp reached into his pocket, pulling forth a small pistol. He aimed it straight at my heart.

"You'll be first, I think, being the more annoying of the pair."

The shot went off and I flew to the side. I stumbled, looking down, expecting to see blood spilling from my chest. There was nothing. Next to me, Dove fell to the ground with a thud. She had pushed me out of the way.

Timothy Sharp was pulling back the hammer of his pistol. Without thinking, I bolted toward him. Before he could get the second shot off, I slammed into him with the force of everything I had. He stumbled backward, the shock of what I'd done clear on his face. There was no stopping me now. I would not lie down for this man who had taken so much from me and everything from those poor men.

While he was confused, I grabbed for the gun, wrenching his hand back unnaturally until he yelped, grabbing at my hair with his free hand. He could pull all the hair from my head if he wished, I wasn't about to let go of that gun. I crooked up my knee and sent it straight between his legs.

"Dammit," he yelped again, doubling over and releasing the gun.

I turned it on him, in complete disbelief that somehow I had gotten the upper hand. I needed to check on Dove, but I couldn't give up my advantage. I wouldn't even risk one glance back at her. Tears spilled down my face. She sacrificed herself for me.

"I should shoot you where you stand, I hate you that much. Lucky for you, you and I aren't cut from the same cloth."

I stood there, pistol gripped in my hand, wondering what I should do next. Sharp laughed, breathy and pained. "You better shoot me. How else do you think you'll get out of here, little girl?"

Anger flashed through my skull. Without warning, as I had done to him, Timothy Sharp rushed me. There was only reaction as I squeezed the trigger.

Sharp crumpled into a ball at the same time as he fell. He rolled over on his side, blood pouring onto the boards of the floor. I backed away, not trusting enough to turn my back on him. When I reached Dove, I knelt, the gun still clutched in one hand. She, too, had rolled on her side.

"Dove," I whispered, rolling her onto her back.

Her eyes were open, and she was breathing. Her hand clutched her side, blood streaming down her dress. She looked at me. "I think it went through me." Her voice was strained, thin.

I moved her hand, trying to look and keep an eye on Sharp. I'd never felt such relief in my life. "It looks like a graze mark. Oh, thank God. Here." I set down the pistol long enough to tear a strip from the bottom of my dress. "Hold this over it tight. I don't care how much it hurts, press it hard. Do you understand?"

Dove nodded, wincing as I pressed the fabric into her wound.

"What in God's name has happened here?" I heard Tesla before I saw him. Never had I felt so relieved.

"You'll never believe it."

CHAPTER TWENTY-TWO

Sharp was dead. There was nothing to be done for him. I didn't have the time to think too much on what I'd done. Right now, I needed to get Dove to Dr. Miller.

I quickly gave Tesla the rundown of events as he and I managed to get Dove on her feet and on the back of Lady.

"I'll get Dove to the doctor. You go for the police," I said, mounting my horse while trying not to jostle Dove too much. She hadn't spoken once. Her face was becoming paler, sicklier by the second. I was afraid if I didn't get her to Dr. Miller soon, she would lose too much blood. For now, she seemed to be holding on.

I pulled Lady out of the yard; Dove collapsed against my back. She lightly placed her free hand around my waist. I pulled it tighter around me. "Hold on tight. We're going to get there as quickly as possible. I'm afraid this is going to hurt."

"It can't hurt more than it already does. Run, Cora. I'll keep hold."

Run, we did. Dove moaned behind me with every step Lady took, but we were stopping in front of Dr. Miller's after only ten minutes. Sliding off Lady, Dove fell in a heap in the freshly turned dirt. I jumped down, yelling as loud as

I could for help. She was losing consciousness. Getting her inside would require help.

The strange man who had led me and Marshall into Dr. Miller's study came running down the walk. "She's been shot. The bullet grazed her side," I explained as he scooped Dove into his arms. Her head lolled, eyes rolling back in her head.

We were inside the dirty hallway, making tracks toward a room just beyond the doctor's office. This room was clean, sterile. A plain, single bed with clean white sheets sat in the middle of the room. The man laid Dove gently on top of this as Dr. Miller appeared.

"What's happened, Cora?" he asked as he rushed to the basin to wash his hands. Dr. Miller rolled up the sleeves of his nightshirt.

"She was shot by her fiancé. The bullet grazed her side. I don't think it's inside her."

If Dr. Miller was shocked by my words, he didn't show it. He bent over Dove, removed the torn bit of silk soaked through with bright-red blood, and threw it in a bowl on the floor. I stood by helplessly as the doctor and his assistant tore off a good portion of Dove's dress to expose the horrible gash. Gawking at the wound was only making me queasy, so while the men worked, I closed my eyes.

I thought back on the events of the past few days. It seemed like an eternity since Joe Williams had died, setting off the string of events I hoped were now at an end. Dove moaned on the bed. Dr. Miller's assistant took a bottle from the metal cabinetry. He poured some of its liquid into a cloth and placed the cloth over Dove's mouth and nose. She quieted down again.

"The good news, Cora, is this wound isn't serious."

I slumped against the closed door, my hands covering the tears spilling down my cheeks.

"Don't worry. She'll have a nasty scar, and she'll be sore for some time. But she's young and strong. She'll be fine. Why don't you wait in my office?"

I did more than wait, I fell asleep. Curled up on a settee in the corner of the warm room, I blacked out the second my eyes closed.

When I woke, the room was crowded with bodies. Mother sat in a chair, holding my hand. Dr. Miller sat at his desk, talking softly with Mr. Tesla, who stood next to his chair. Two police officers milled about. Wolf and Harrison stood side by side, hovering behind me over my shoulder.

Harrison, his brow creased, and his arms crossed, expelled a long breath as our eyes met. "You certainly know how to scare people, Cora." He bent down next to my ear. "But I've never been so happy to see someone wake up."

I wanted to feel lighthearted and happy to see him. My mind was elsewhere.

Mother increased the pressure on my hand, bringing my attention back around to her. "You're probably anxious about Dove. Poor thing is out of danger. She's under arrest, but she's resting in the next room." My mother knew my first thoughts would be of my friend. "These men would like to speak with you about all that's happened."

My gaze swept the room, landing on Wolf, who gave me a wink. "I'll leave, I just wanted to make sure you were okay. Please do us all a favor and don't ever put yourself in the path of a killer again."

I tried to smile at my old friend. Instead, my mind was marred by the events of last night. Thoughts of Dove covered in blood, the struggle with Timothy Sharp, and how the gun felt in my hand. Pulling that trigger was a horrible thing. When would the sound of the gunshot cease to reverberate through my skull?

I gave my account, one officer scribbling away as I talked, the other staring at me as if he couldn't quite believe all I said. The story was true, every word.

EPILOGUE

Dove bustled about her room, head down, as she packed her trunks. This was the first time I'd been alone with her since the trial. Maxwell Priest was immediately released after the fight of my life inside Tesla's experimental lab. Dove made her statement against Timothy Sharp and all he had done. Dove then confessed to poisoning the police officer with the Spanish fly. The one thing she had been able to tamper with, the man's supply of meat, poisoned him slowly over the course of several days, until he finally ate the last of it in his stew. The stew had been the last straw for the officer's compromised system. Captain King wanted very much to put Dove behind bars, but after a visit from Dove's father and several prominent men in town, including General Palmer, he and the judge settled on probation. Tesla's documents were recovered, and life was returning to normal.

"South Carolina will be lovely this time of year." I tried to make small talk, unsure of our relationship for the first time in all my seventeen years. Dove was going to Charleston to live with her grandmother for an undetermined amount of time. I couldn't very well see her returning to Colorado Springs any time soon. She felt as if she had become a pariah in this town, and she wasn't wrong. I couldn't imagine our friends and neighbors ever forgetting what she had done.

"I suppose," she said softly, her back to me. She stopped in the middle of folding chemises, her shoulders moving up and down with the tears she quietly shed.

I sprang up from my seat. "Dove, I would love to visit you, if I could. I've never been to the South, and I'm going to miss you so very much."

I turned her toward me. Dove dissolved into loud sobs against my shoulder. It was all I could do to keep some composure.

"Thank you for not hating me, Cora. I don't know what I would've done had you despised me."

"I could never hate you, not for any reason. You didn't know what would happen."

I left Dove to finish her packing with a promise to see her off in the morning. Feeling sad at heart, I walked back to my house.

A man stood out front, next to his horse, sugar cubes in his hands.

"Don't feed him too many. You'll make him sick," I said as I walked up to Harrison.

He was leaning back on one foot in a way that conveyed he hadn't a care in the world. I wished I could have felt the same. That one lock of hair tumbled down low over his eye. Those amber eyes glowed with a mischievous smirk. "Don't worry, there's plenty for you."

I laughed. "No, thank you."

"Let's go for a ride, Cora. You need to be out in the sunshine. It's a beautiful day." He was right about that. For the first time, I noticed the unseasonably warm weather. Birds chirped from the top of the trees. I would gladly ride with Harrison to the ends of the earth. "You'll be happy to know that I spoke to Mr. Tesla about Mr. Hill. Tesla is going to speak with the school board about keeping Mr. Hill on, while making accommodations for his knees."

This was the best news I'd heard in a while. I looked at Harrison, really looked at him. He had been there for me in so many ways over the past several days. Yes, his initial motives were singularly romantic, but I didn't mind. Not now.

"First things, first." I stepped in front of him, so close I could hear his breath.

"This time, I'm ready." He grinned that infuriatingly beautiful grin as he reached an arm around my waist. He drew me even nearer. Harrison gripped my waist, our faces inches apart, and brushed a strand of stray hair over my ear. This time, the chill that ran down my back was one of pleasure, not the terror I had become accustomed to.

Harrison left his hand on the side of my face. I closed my eyes, ready for what I knew would come next. The second I felt the pressure of his mouth on mine, I no longer knew myself. I threw my arms around him, pressing my body closer into his. Our mouths parted, tongues exploring with gentle passion.

"You continue to surprise me, Cora Croft," Harrison mumbled, his breath hot against my lips.

"Stick around, you never know what I'll do next."

AUTHOR'S NOTE

This novel was born out of my deep affection for my hometown of Colorado Springs, and its fascinating history. I am continually inspired by Colorado.

Thank you so much to my husband, Brian, for always being in my corner, and thank you to our son for being the best kid around.

Thank you to the editor of this book, Yezanira Venecia and Melissa Keir at Inkspell Publishing for helping bring this book to life.

If you've enjoyed this book, or any book, please leave a quick review. Reviews help authors in more ways than one and are truly appreciated.

FALL IN LOVE WITH THE IMMORTAL KINDRED SERIES, FEATURING HISTORICAL EVENTS WOVEN THROUGH A VAMPIRE ROMANCE.

Deepest Midnight

True love never dies.

For Millicent, a once French noblewoman turned immortal vampire, forever is a long time to live in despair. The love of her life is murdered the night she becomes immortal. Millicent spends her endless night in a melancholy which never ends. Two hundred forty years later, she locks eyes with an English actor, who happens to look exactly like her long dead love.

Sadness turns to happiness as Millicent and Jack find passion in each other's arms. Their fling quickly turns serious as Millicent finds happiness once again—and possibly her one true love.

However, their relationship becomes complicated

by her own uncertainty, Jack's mortality, and the other man in Millicent's life, Alexandre, her maker and companion. When Alexandre puts his foot down, Millicent must decide if she's going to continue to be led by others or take the reins and drive the outcome of her life.

Deepest Midnight is set in modern day Savannah, Ga with occasional glimpses back to 18ᵗʰ century France. This is the first book in The Immortal Kindred Series.

Rebel Heart

Always and Forever

Annie is a Culper Spy captured by Hessian soldiers. Powerful and mysterious Captain Thayer Emmerich takes mercy and releases her. Annie is inexplicably drawn to the handsome German, but she hates the feeling of powerlessness the enemy has left her with. Annie would give anything to be stronger.

One evening at the famous Green Dragon Tavern,

Annie befriends the ethereal Millicent. Soon after meeting Millicent, Annie discovers her secret--her new friend isn't human. Millicent introduces Annie to her maker, Alexandre, and Annie joins their preternatural family.

Annie finally has the strength and freedom she needs to aid the revolution and see Thayer, once again. The two discover a passion neither has known before. But, too many complications exist for the pair to find happily ever after. Not only are they fighting on opposite sides of the war, the evil Emilia Romanov has plans for Thayer that do not include a love affair.

Rebel Heart is set in 18ᵗʰ century Boston and Savannah, as well as modern day Germany and France. This is the second book in The Immortal Kindred Series.

The King of Kings

Love has no limits…
Alexandre has retreated from the world. He has no

one to love, nowhere to call home. While licking his wounds in the middle of nowhere, Alexandre is approached by Irish lass, Bria. She has a proposal for him; to follow her to Ireland and fight demons.

Alexandre finds this amusing, but intriguing. More than anything, he is curious to see the individual who sent Bria, someone from his ancient past.

In Ireland, Alexandre confronts a dilemma greater than fighting demons. He must face down fiends of all kinds, deciding once and for all who he really is. Sparks fly between Bria and Alexandre, adding to the already complicated situation. Can a bad boy vampire really change?

The King of Kings is set in southern Ireland with a glimpse back to Ancient Egypt.

Goddess of the Moon

An impossible attraction. An apocalyptic threat.
After vanquishing a Celtic death demon, Selene should be kicking back and enjoying some free time. However, her

life is anything but relaxed. She must travel to Romania, the last place she'd ever thought she'd be, facing another demon threat. Just another day at the office for the daughter of Cleopatra.

The situation soon escalates. The simple problem Selene thought she was facing, becomes intense--FAST. The dilemma is much greater than she initially feared. Throw in a sexy witch she doesn't want to be attracted to, and her life really gets complicated.

Overconfidence leads Selene to make a mistake which could cost everything. Can she unravel the mystery before it's too late? Or will her latest nemesis be the death of her and those she loves?

Goddess of the Moon is the fourth book of The Immortal Kindred Series and is set primarily in Brasov, Romania.

Dark Star

The compelling final story in the enchanting series which began with Deepest Midnight....

The Immortal Kindred gather together as chaos erupts.

Two of their own have gone missing, sucked back in time. Vampire demigod Selene messed with the wrong goddess of death. Now they're all in danger.

Millicent and Annie come face to face with the distant past. No longer immortal, they must draw on their inner strength to see them through travails long thought dead and buried. Tash, the witch, draws on every spell he knows to bring the women home as he taps into the power of the dark star.

Will it be enough to grant the immortals their happily ever after? Will the goddess, Nephthys, put an end to everything they know and love?

Dark Star is an epic adventure that will take you all over the globe and through time itself.

Available at all major book retailers

ABOUT THE AUTHOR

A.D. Brazeau is an award-winning author who writes what she loves. From dark and fantastical fairytale retellings to quirky romance, and everything in between, she loves nothing more than to immerse herself in new worlds. A.D. Brazeau is a book-obsessed wife, mother, and dog lover, who grew up surrounded by stories. Not much has changed. A.D. is from Colorado Springs, Co.